ALSO BY ROLAND SMITH

THE CRYPTID HUNTERS BOOKS
Cryptid Hunters
Tentacles

THE I, Q BOOKS
I, Q: Independence Hall
I, Q: The White House

THE JACK OSBORNE BOOKS
Zach's Lie
Jack's Run

THE JACOB LANSA BOOKS
Thunder Cave
Jaguar
The Last Lobo

OTHER NOVELS BY THE AUTHOR
The Captain's Dog
Elephant Run
Peak
Sasquatch
Storm Runners

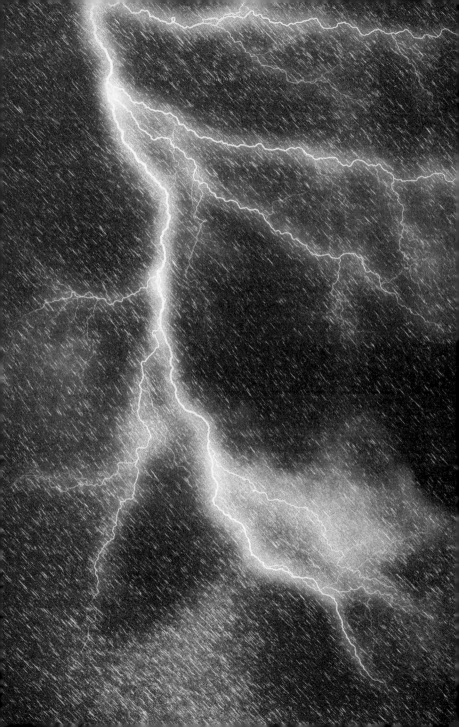

STORM RUNNERS
THE SURGE

ROLAND SMITH

SCHOLASTIC PRESS

NEW YORK

ISBN 978-0-545-39462-8

10 9 8 7 6 5 4 3 2 1   11 12 13 14 15

Printed in the U.S.A.   40

This edition first printing, September 2011

Book design by Phil Falco

FOR CHAD MYERS,
THE GUY I TUNE IN TO DURING
WEATHER DISASTERS

12 HOURS

Chase Masters looked at his watch. It was hard to believe it had only been twelve hours since he, Nicole, and Rashawn had gotten on the ill-fated school bus at Palm Breeze Middle School.

During those terrible hours, the bus had sunk, its driver had died, and they had nearly drowned. Chase had broken a front tooth, his shoulder had been smashed by a falling chunk of asphalt road, and a thirteen-foot alligator had attacked him.

But we're alive, *he thought.* Hurricane Emily didn't get us . . .

The wind slammed into the side of the metal barn where they had taken shelter.

. . . yet.

Rashawn and Nicole jumped.

"What time is it?" *Nicole asked with a nervous laugh.*

Chase told her. . . .

03:51 AM

"Sounds like we're trapped in a steel barrel and someone's poundin' on the side with a sledgehammer," Rashawn said, covering her ears.

That's exactly what it sounds like, Chase thought, tempted to find a steel barrel, curl up inside, and stay there until Hurricane Emily blew herself out. He ran his tongue along the jagged edge of his front tooth and stretched his shoulder — both still ached. He'd hoped that when they finally reached the farm the nightmare would be over, but it wasn't. A leopard named Hector was running around the property with Nicole's grandmother's pet monkey, Poco, dangling from his mouth, and her family's house looked like it had been crushed with a wrecking ball. At first they'd thought that Nicole's grandmother, Momma Rossi, had been trapped under the rubble, but she had taken refuge down the hill in the barn just before the house collapsed.

Momma Rossi was a little person, like Nicole's father, Marco. The dwarfism gene had bypassed Nicole, so she was regular height. Chase glanced at Rashawn, who was alternating her gaze between Momma Rossi and the very large elephant chained in the middle of a sawdust-covered circus ring. It was hard to say which sight confused Rashawn more.

Momma Rossi fixed her brown eyes on Chase. "How are my treasures?"

"Uh . . . I don't know. I didn't get a chance to check," he replied. Momma Rossi had predicted that the house would go down in the storm. A day earlier, she'd asked Chase to transfer dozens of boxes of memorabilia to a storage container near the swimming pool in back of the house. He'd caulked the container and wrapped it in tarps, but he doubted it had held up to Hurricane Emily's fury.

"What's important is that you're all okay," Momma Rossi said.

"What *is* this place?" Rashawn asked.

"Our farm is winter quarters for the Rossi Brothers' Circus," Momma Rossi explained. "Normally this time of year the farm would be filled with show animals and performers, but they managed to book some additional dates in Mexico, prolonging the season. Nicole's mother runs the show and her father — my son — Marco runs the farm."

"Why'd this elephant stay behind?"

"Pet? She's pregnant with her first calf," Momma Rossi said.

"Why's she chained up?"

"So she doesn't float to the ceiling," Nicole and Chase said in unison and laughed.

"You guys are hilarious," Rashawn said, rolling her eyes. "I bet she's chained so she doesn't tear this building down."

"You're right," Nicole said. "We don't have an elephant-proof building. The show elephants spend their winters in Texas with our trainer. Pet would be there now, but we didn't want to move her this close to having her calf."

"I hope the building is hurricane-proof," Rashawn said.

Chase had never been in a hurricane, but he'd seen plenty of dangerous weather. Following his father from disaster to disaster the past two years had shown him that no building was stormproof.

At that moment something heavy slammed into the side of the metal circus barn. They all jumped.

"What was that?" Rashawn shouted.

"I don't know," Nicole said. "But it sounded like it was shot out of a cannon at point-blank range."

"Storm debris," Chase said. "Probably from the house. It's upwind." By the loudness and density of the hit, he thought it might be one of the house's toilets. His father was always giving him articles about people getting killed by unusual WPPs, wind-propelled projectiles. "I think we'll be —"

The first thud was followed by a salvo of WPPs. Everyone covered their ears and backed away from the wall. Nicole huddled closer to her grandmother, and Rashawn was shaking. Chase stood frozen in place. The barrage went on for several minutes, then suddenly stopped.

They all stared at the wall. No one spoke. The wind still rattled the metal building, but the sound was nothing compared to the strikes they'd just heard.

Nicole broke the silence. "That was insane!"

"I thought the wall was going to fall down right on top of us," Rashawn said.

"So did I," Chase admitted. He walked up to the wall and checked for damage. There were a lot of dents, but nothing seemed to have pierced the metal. "Heavy-gauge steel," he said, not mentioning that if one of the panels had come loose, it would have peeled off the building like the skin from a rotten banana, with the other panels close behind. "We're safe in here," he added with more confidence than he felt.

"Are you sure?" Nicole asked.

Her long black hair was wet and tangled with twigs and dirt. Her usually bright brown eyes were dull with fatigue. Chase wasn't surprised, after the terrifying journey they'd endured to get to the farm. "Maybe you should sit down," he said.

"He's right," Momma Rossi said. "You look dead on your feet."

Nicole nodded and collapsed on the curb of the circus ring. "I am. That last swim took a lot out of me." She looked up at Chase. "You haven't answered my question."

"I don't know if we're safe or not," Chase admitted. "There's water coming in around the door, which isn't surprising with this wind and rain. I guess I'd better check out the rest of the building, but to do that I'll need more light."

"Our generator can only power one of these rings at a time," Nicole said. "I don't know how to switch it to the other rings." She looked at her grandmother.

"I don't know either," Momma Rossi said. "The lights were on over Pet's ring when I got into here."

"I'll check it out," Chase said. "Where's the generator?"

"In the workshop — connected to the bunkhouse," Momma Rossi said.

Chase clicked on his headlamp and shined the beam along the wall. "Battery's just about gone." He checked the second headlamp. Its beam was worse.

Momma Rossi took a flashlight out of her coat pocket. "Plenty of life left in this one. You should find batteries in the bunkhouse. I'm not sure where they keep them. If you don't find them in the kitchen, check in the workshop. Marco's been camping out in the bunkhouse for the last week to stay close to Pet. There should be plenty of food in the kitchen if any of you are hungry."

"We haven't eaten for hours," Chase said. "I'll see what I can find."

"Do you think *your* dad can find *my* dad?" Nicole asked.

"If I can get ahold of him." Chase pulled a plastic bag from his cargo pocket. Inside was a satellite phone just like the one his father and his father's partner, Tomás, carried. Chase's phone had died after the school bus sank, but it had come back to life just before they reached the farm. He'd been able to talk to his father long enough to find out that he and Tomás were stranded on the other side of the lake and were looking for a way around to reach the farm. Chase did not expect to see them anytime soon. He pushed the on button. Nothing happened.

"Still dead," Chase said.

Momma Rossi had set up a small electric heater next to the ring. Chase removed the phone battery, wiped it and the phone off as best as he could, then set both of them near the heater.

Tears formed in Nicole's eyes. "I hope Dad's not hurt."

"Marco is fine," Momma Rossi said, putting her arms around her granddaughter.

"Are you just saying that to make me feel better?" Nicole asked. "Or do you know?"

"I know," Momma Rossi said. "Just like I knew you and Chase and Rashawn were in danger."

Just like she knew the farmhouse was going to blow over and nobody believed her, Chase thought. *Just like she knew that Mom and Monica had died in a car crash on a mountain.*

"Excuse me, ma'am," Rashawn said.

"Please call me Momma Rossi."

"Okay, Momma Rossi. No disrespect, but I just met you a few minutes ago when we stepped into this barn. How could you know about me before then?"

Momma Rossi smiled, but didn't answer her.

Chase looked at Rashawn. "She just knows things. Do you want to help me check out the rest of this barn?"

"Sure," Rashawn said. "But first I want to know if Momma Rossi has a bag of rice in that kitchen of hers."

"I'm sure there is, dear," Momma Rossi said. "But we don't have any way to cook it with the power out."

"I don't want to eat it," Rashawn said. "I want to use it on Chase's sat phone. My daddy is always dunkin' his cell phone in the water — he manages a wildlife refuge, so he's outside all day. He just puts it in a bag of uncooked rice and the grains suck the moisture right out of it. Couple hours, the phone's good as new."

"You're kidding," Chase said.

"No joke," Rashawn said. "And when you get that phone fired up, you also need to ask your daddy about *my* daddy. I'm sure he's out looking for me too."

"I will," Chase promised.

04:12 AM

Chase led Rashawn into the dark shadows of the circus barn. He didn't really need her help, but he wanted to give Nicole and Momma Rossi some time to themselves. Also, Rashawn knew things he didn't. She might *see* things he didn't as he checked the barn for hurricane damage. He'd only met Rashawn a few hours ago, but she had proven herself over and over again, just as Nicole had.

There were three brightly colored, curbed circus rings running down the middle of the barn. Each ring was at least three hundred feet across. Pet was chained in the center of the first ring, and stretched across the second, several feet off the ground, was a gigantic net. Thirty feet above the net, a tightrope connected two platforms. Next to the tightrope was an array of trapeze equipment.

Chase shined his light up at the ceiling. A series of catwalks crisscrossed the rafters above the equipment.

"What are those for?" Rashawn asked.

"They must use them to adjust the rigging and the lights," Chase said.

Rashawn jumped up and brushed the bottom of the net with her hand. "Guess this is in case someone does a header from that wire or a swing. When we get to the bunkhouse, I'm going to find me a blanket, climb up on this net, and sleep for a week. It's like a big ol' hammock."

Chase smiled. Another thing he liked about Rashawn was her ability to joke when there was nothing to joke about. He cut across the ring to the north wall of the building and put his hands on the metal sheeting. It was vibrating in the wind, but there was no evidence of water getting in. The wind was blowing from the west, where they had entered the building, which accounted for the water pooling inside the door near the elephant ring. The fact that there was no water along this wall gave him hope that the building might hold up to Hurricane Emily. He crossed to the opposite wall, but it was blocked off by a stack of hay bales that reached almost to the rafters.

Chase and Rashawn walked down to the third ring, which held a circular cage. "I think they use this one to train the big cats," Chase said.

"How many cats do they have?" Rashawn asked.

"I'm not exactly sure," Chase said. "When I got here, Nicole showed me five lions and a leopard."

"The one named Hector?" Rashawn asked.

"Yeah. He was confiscated from a drug dealer and he's very aggressive."

"Don't you think all leopards are aggressive?"

"Good point," Chase said.

"You think the lions were born free like Hector?"

"I hope not." Chase neglected to tell her that the biggest lion, Simba, had been retired from the show the previous year after mauling his trainer.

"How come you didn't tell Momma Rossi about the dead monkey Hector was trotting around with in his mouth? Poco, right?"

"Right," Chase answered. "It's not my place to tell her. The last time I saw Poco, he was in Momma Rossi's kitchen wearing tiny diapers and eating sweet potato peels — he's her pet. I'm sure Nicole will tell her when the time is right."

"They make monkey diapers?"

"I'm guessing that Momma Rossi makes monkey diapers."

"Never heard of such a thing." Rashawn glanced back at the lighted end of the long barn. "Is Momma Rossi psychic or something?"

"I guess we'll find out," Chase said.

04:19 AM

"We can't stay here," Chase's father, John Masters, announced. He was looking at the display of his handheld GPS. "The question is, where do we go and how do we get there from here?"

Here was a two-lane country road about three miles from the same lake Chase's school bus had sunk into several hours earlier.

Chase and his friends are lucky to have survived, John thought. *If they made it to the Rossis' farm. If they're still alive.*

John Masters had tried to call Chase a half a dozen times since their garbled sat phone conversation more than an hour ago. There had been no answer. The eye of the storm had passed over, and by the look of things inside the 4x4 truck he was sitting in, the back end of Hurricane Emily was going to be just as bad as — if not worse than — the front.

Something large, heavy, and black bounced off the hood of the truck.

Maybe a lot worse, John thought.

"What was that?" Mark shouted from the crew cab behind John.

"Tree stump," John said. "I think."

"It felt like a meteorite!" Mark was a cameraman from a local TV station in Saint Petersburg, Florida.

Sitting between John and his partner, Tomás, on the front seat was Cindy Stewart, a TV reporter who worked with Mark. John still wasn't sure why he had invited Cindy and Mark to drive along with him and Tomás into the center of the worst hurricane in U.S. history. They had already crashed and totaled one truck, and if they didn't get moving, the second truck was going to be history as well, along with its four occupants.

Cindy looked at the photographs stuck to Tomás's dashboard. "Are these your children, Tomás?"

"*Sí.*" Tomás smiled and listed their names as he pointed at each photo. "And my wife, Guadalupe."

"Are they here in the States?"

Tomás shook his gray head. "Mexico. I see them one time every year."

"You must miss them."

"*Sí.* Of course."

"Why don't you bring them up here?"

"Guadalupe, she loves our village in the mountains. Too expensive here with so many children."

Tomás had been working for John Masters for more than twenty years. When John sold his part of the family construction business to his brother-in-law and hit the road to chase storms, there was no question about Tomás going with him. They were closer than brothers.

John stared straight ahead through the windshield. The path before them looked more like a stream than a road, and it was strewn with downed trees as far as he could see. With the gale-force winds pushing the water, it was impossible to tell which way it was flowing, but one thing was clear: The water was rising. They had to get to high ground. Soon.

"The surge," John said.

"What?" Mark shouted above the roaring wind.

"Storm surge," John clarified. "Flooding. It could cause more damage than the wind."

"After what we've already been through, I'd prefer not to drown if it's okay with you," Mark called from his spot in the back.

"I'll see what I can do." John leaned over Cindy and showed the GPS to Tomás.

"We can try," Tomás said, after studying the map.

"Try what?" Cindy asked.

"A detour." John leaned back into his seat and put his seat belt on. The 4x4 rocked as Tomás pulled it off the road and headed into the woods.

"What's he doing?" Mark shouted, struggling to get his seat belt on as he bounced in the jump seat like a tennis ball.

"Trying to save you from death by drowning," John said. "There's a rail line about a mile away. It should be dry and clear of downed trees. If we can reach it and get the rig up on the bed, it'll take us to the main highway."

"So now it's death by oncoming train," Mark said.

"Trains don't run during hurricanes," John said. "But there are any number of other things that could kill us on the way."

"Like death by flying tree stump," Cindy said.

"Yep, that's one of them," John said. Then he proceeded to give them a grim list of death by WPPs.

04:25 AM

A blast of windblown rain knocked Chase and Rashawn backward as they opened the bunkhouse door.

"Window!" Chase shouted. "Over the sink!"

They hunkered down and fought their way across the room toward the opening. The window was broken. Chase grabbed a large wooden cutting board from the kitchen counter. With the wind and rain hammering their faces, it took all of their strength to wedge the board into the window frame.

"It will keep most of the rain out," Chase said, out of breath.

Rashawn leaned against the counter and wrung the water out of her hair. "And I was just getting dry!"

Chase shined the flashlight at the four inches of water covering the floor. An armada of plastic cups and containers bobbed on the surface like little ships. He walked cautiously to the center of the room.

"What are you doing?" Rashawn asked.

Instead of answering, Chase bent down and pulled up a large frying pan by the handle. With the drain unplugged the water level started to drop.

"Cement floor," Chase said. "Three-inch central drain. Shouldn't be too much damage after it dries."

"What is it with you?" Rashawn asked.

"What do you mean?"

"'Cement floor. Three-inch central drain . . .' You sound like an architect or something. And before our bus ran off the road and sank, you sounded like you worked for FEMA. I'm not complaining, but what kind of kid carries a satellite phone, several bottles of water, two headlamps, and a first aid kit to school in his backpack?"

"A very strange kid," Chase admitted, and then gave her a brief outline of what had happened to him the past two years. He finished just as the last of the water circled the drain.

"I'm sorry about your momma and sister, Chase," Rashawn said. "The last couple of years of your life sound like the water goin' down this drain."

Chase smiled. "You're right. It has kind of sucked."

"Your daddy really got hit by a lightning bolt?"

"It went right through his shoulder. Blew his boots off his feet. He was in a coma for days. When he came out of it he looked like my father, but it was like someone else had crawled into his skin."

"So now he and this Tomás guy drive around the country looking for storm damage, then charge people an arm and a leg to fix things. And drag you along with them."

"Yup, that's M.D. Emergency Services," Chase said.

"M.D., like in doctor?"

Chase shook his head. "M.D., like in *Masters of Disaster*."

"At least your daddy has a sense of humor."

"Not really," Chase said. "Not anymore. But he's a good contractor and he's taught me a lot."

"What happens to you after Emily blows through?"

"Hopefully we'll stick around awhile. I like it here. But my father doesn't spend too much time in one spot."

"Your daddy sounds a lot like *my* daddy. I bet my daddy's worked at a dozen wildlife refuges from here to Oregon. Our last name is Stone. Momma calls him Mr. Rollin' Stone, but I think she likes movin' around just as much he does." Rashawn glanced at the rain blowing through a gap in the window. "I just hope they had the sense to stay out of this mess and not go out looking for me."

"Do you have brothers or sisters?"

"A little brother, Randall . . . two years old."

"You live on the wildlife refuge?"

"Smack-dab in the middle of it. The job always comes with a house."

"A sturdy house?"

Rashawn laughed. "Brick. I made fun of it when we moved in. Called it the Three Little Pigs' House. If it's standing when this is over and my family's okay, I won't be making fun of that house anymore."

"I think they'll be fine. I'm sure your parents have seen plenty of bad weather living out in the woods."

Rashawn stole another glance at the window. "I don't think anybody's seen weather like this before."

"You're probably right," Chase agreed. He switched on the headlamp and handed it to her. "Not much light. Think you can manage to find some batteries while I look for the generator?"

"No problem," Rashawn said, slipping the headlamp over her forehead. "I'll raid the cupboards for food too, and find some rice for that satellite phone of yours."

Chase shined his light around the room, which was a lot bigger and nicer than he'd expected. It was a combination kitchen/recreation room. The kitchen was equipped with shiny stainless steel appliances, granite countertops, and a commercial refrigerator big enough to hang a cow in. The recreation room had a pool table, leather sofas and chairs, and two gigantic flat-screen TVs.

"Whoa!" Rashawn said. "When Momma Rossi said 'bunkhouse' I was thinking bunk beds, cowboys, and a potbellied ol' stove . . . but this is nice! Makes me want to switch my dream of becoming a biologist like my daddy and join the circus instead."

Chase smiled. He'd said almost the same thing to Nicole the day before. He opened the door to the right of the recreation room. It led to a hallway with several doors running along the left side and another door at the end. As he walked down the hall, he tried the doors on the left and found them all locked except for one. It opened into a furnished apartment with a sitting room, a bedroom, and a bathroom. There were no personal effects, which led Chase to believe the locked doors were for occupied apartments.

The Rossis take good care of their roughnecks, he thought.

He continued down to the door at the end, which opened onto the workshop. Like the kitchen/recreation room and the apartments, it wasn't what he'd expected. It was almost as big as the circus barn, well equipped, and immaculately clean. With the assortment of tools hanging above the long workbench, the roughnecks could repair anything. Along another wall were three garage doors rattling loudly in the wind, each big enough to back a semitrailer through.

The generator was in the corner along the common wall between the barn and the workshop. Chase knew the generator was on by the green light, but he couldn't hear it above the wind. He walked over and checked the gas. It was close to empty. He picked up the gas can next to it and his heart sank. It was completely dry, as were the two other cans he found along the wall. It took him nearly twenty minutes to discover that there wasn't a drop of gasoline in the workshop.

Rashawn came in with her headlamp shining brightly again.

"I see you found batteries," Chase shouted above the rumbling garage doors.

"And food, and blankets, and pillows, and towels, and a bag of rice for that phone of yours."

"Good job," he said, then frowned.

"Everything okay?" she asked.

"Yeah," Chase said, although he knew it wouldn't be okay if he didn't find some gasoline. In a little while it was going to be as dark inside the barn as a mine shaft. Chase looked at his watch. It was 5:01 AM.

05:01AM

Tomás's 4x4 bouncing along the slick railroad ties was like an amusement park ride for the occupants — minus the amusement.

"How much farther?" Mark shouted from the jump seat in back, where he was getting the brunt of the bounce.

"About half a mile," John shouted back.

"How far have we gone?"

"About a half a mile."

"You gotta be kidding me! I'm getting pounded back here. I need a helmet!"

John turned. Mark was cradling the video camera like it was an infant. "You might want to let go of that camera and hang on."

"This camera is worth more than my life."

"It doesn't even belong to you," Cindy pointed out. "The station owns it."

"Yeah, but if I break it, I *will* own it," Mark said. "And a busted camera won't do me much good considering that in a couple hours, when I don't show up at the station for work, I'll be unemployed."

"So will I," Cindy said.

Cindy and Mark had both known when they climbed into John Masters's truck and headed toward Hurricane Emily that there was a good chance they would not make it back to Saint Petersburg by morning. Cindy had accepted John's invitation because, after spending half the previous day watching him work, she was curious about him. Mark had tagged along because he was curious about the hurricane. They had both gotten what they wanted. Cindy had interviewed John during the terrifying ride into the storm, and she'd learned enough about him to know that he would make a very interesting subject of a documentary. She was thinking of calling it *The Man Who Got Struck by Lightning*. Mark had shot some amazing footage of Emily's fury, but the only way to save his job was to get that footage on the air. Without power there was no way to do this.

"It was a lousy television station anyway," Cindy said. "Look on the bright side. We won't have to put up with Richard Krupp anymore."

Richard Krupp was the station's lead anchorman and the most popular television personality in Saint Petersburg.

"It'll be nice not to have to deal with that gasbag anymore," Mark admitted. "But how am I going to make a living?"

"With me," Cindy said. "We'll go freelance."

"Without a camera?"

"I have some money put away. I'll get you a camera. In the meantime hand the station's camera up front. We'll hang on to it while you get a grip."

Mark happily gave Cindy and John the expensive camera to guard for a while.

John looked over at Tomás, who was hunched over the steering wheel, trying to see through the watery windshield. He'd offered to take over the driving again, but Tomás shook his head just as he had every time John had suggested it.

Three minutes later they hit something lying across the track. The truck went airborne, rolled counterclockwise, slammed back onto the track on the driver's side, then slid for thirty feet between the rails, with the air bags deployed, before coming to a teetering stop.

"Is everyone okay?" John asked.

"I'm good," Cindy said.

"Okay," Tomás said.

"Soiled underpants," Mark said.

"Too much information," Cindy said.

"How's the camera?" Mark asked.

"It's jammed between Tomás's shoulder and my ear," Cindy answered. "But I think it's fine."

"Put it in park, Tomás," John said. "Don't turn the engine off. We may not be able to get it started again."

"That seems moot since the truck is lying on its side," Mark said.

"With some luck we might be able to right it," John said. "I'm going to try to climb out through the window. Nobody move. I don't want to flip it over on the roof, on top of me, or over the trestle."

"As in bridge?" Mark asked.

"I can't see very clearly through the windshield, but it looks like this section of track is ten to twelve feet above a swamp. If we go into the drink, we'll be on foot."

"Providing we don't drown," Mark added.

"Exactly."

"Just so you know, I can't swim."

"That's good to know."

John slipped his headlamp on and opened the passenger window. When he stuck his head outside, the wind nearly pulled him out of the cab.

05:13 AM

Chase put the battery back into the satellite phone, then turned it on.

"No go," he said.

"Rice time." Rashawn took the phone and put it into a Ziploc bag filled with uncooked rice. "You'll be talking to your dad before you know it."

"I hope it works," Nicole said.

"I've never seen this fail." Rashawn started unloading the other goodies from the large box she'd brought from the bunkhouse kitchen.

Chase looked at the electric heater, then at Momma Rossi. "Maybe we should switch the heater off to conserve power."

"Not until you dry off," Momma Rossi said. "How did you and Rashawn get so wet?"

Chase told her about the broken window.

"Did you top the generator off?" Nicole asked.

"I would have, but there wasn't any gas. The cans were all empty." Chase walked over to the heater and put his cold hands in front of it.

"You didn't tell me that," Rashawn said, joining him in front of the heater.

"I thought I'd let everyone know at once." Chase looked at Nicole. "I searched all over the workshop. Is there anyplace else your dad might store it?"

Nicole shook her head. "There are three cans next to the generator. He fills them in town when they're empty."

"There *were* three cans," Chase said. "And they're all empty. Unfortunately, the generator is just about empty too. I'd guess we have about an hour before the lights go off. Maybe less."

"Not good," Nicole said, glancing at Pet. "This barn is dark as a tomb, even during the day." She pointed at a small window to the side of the ring. "That's it for daylight. Dad's been so busy with Pet and taking care of the farm, I guess he forgot to pick up gas."

"You open that big door after sunup," Rashawn said. "There'd be plenty of light."

"The storm might not be over by sunrise," Chase pointed out. "Which would mean no light, or at least not very much."

"And if Pet saw an opening that big," Nicole added, "she'd try to pull her leg off trying to get to it."

"We have plenty of gas in the Shack and Shop," Chase said.

The Shack was the fifth-wheel where Chase and his father lived. The Shop was his father's tractor-trailer rig. It was filled with tools and building supplies. Tomás had a small apartment built into the front end of the Shop.

"You can't go out in this," Nicole said.

"It's either that or we'll be sitting here in the dark *listening* to an elephant being born," Chase said.

"We have flashlights."

"We have one flashlight and two headlamps," Chase corrected. "Which aren't going to do us much good if there's a problem with the calf."

"What about the four-wheeler?" Rashawn said.

"What about it?" Chase asked.

"I don't know what the Shack and Shop is, or where it is, but we rode down here on a four-wheeler and it's parked right outside the door we came through to get into the barn."

Chase smiled. *Rashawn. Always thinking.* He had no desire to fight his way on foot to the Shop to get gas, especially in the dark.

"Is the tank full?" Nicole asked, looking as relieved as he felt.

"Yeah," Chase answered. "Or pretty close to full." One of his father's many rules was that all gas tanks were to be kept full at all times for situations just like this. He had topped the four-wheeler's tank off the previous morning before he'd picked up Nicole and driven her to the road to catch the school bus. "It has a five-gallon tank. We could siphon it into one of the cans and we'd have enough to keep us going for several hours."

"Let's get it inside," Nicole said. "We can crack the big door open and pull it in."

The big door was in fact big enough to drive a semitruck through. But the door wouldn't budge, even with all four of them pushing and pulling on it.

"The wind's too strong out there," Chase said. "We'll never get it open. I'll have to use the small door."

"The four-wheeler won't fit through that door," Nicole said.

"You're right. But I can push it up to the door, and we have to siphon the gas out anyway."

"I'll get the hose and a can," Rashawn said, hurrying off into the darkness toward the bunkhouse.

"That Rashawn's a go-getter," Momma Rossi said. "I like her."

"So do I," Nicole agreed.

"Where does she live?"

"Up the road a few miles. Her dad's the refuge manager."

"We need to turn the heater off," Chase said. "And any lights we don't absolutely need."

Momma Rossi walked over and unplugged the heater. Nicole opened a panel on the wall and switched off everything except for a couple of spotlights over the ring.

A few minutes later, Rashawn returned with a watering hose, an empty gas can, and an armful of pillows and blankets.

"Don't know about you, but I'm going to take a nap after we get the generator gassed up."

"On the big ol' hammock?" Chase asked, taking the gas can from her.

"Yep."

"What are you two talking about?" Nicole asked.

Momma Rossi laughed. "I think they're talking about the catch net for the fliers."

"Fliers?" Rashawn said.

"The trapeze artists," Nicole explained.

Chase took out his pocketknife, cut a length of hose, and walked over to the door with Nicole and Rashawn. "I'll get the four-wheeler as close as I can, and we'll figure out what to do from there. Ready?"

He turned the handle. The door banged open, nearly dislocating his arm. Water and debris flew through the opening.

"Watch out!"

Nicole and Rashawn ducked to either side. Chase dropped to his knees to give the wind a smaller target and peered outside with his headlamp. Shingles, broken furniture, and other house debris lined the outside walls like a four-foot snowdrift of garbage.

WPPs, thought Chase. *We were lucky to get inside the barn when we did.*

The four-wheeler was nowhere to be seen. Chase swore, but the word was lost in the wind. Perhaps more disturbing was the amount of water outside. The side of the barn looked like the bow of a ship slicing through flotsam and jetsam on a rough sea. He pulled his head back inside and struggled to close the door, but could barely move it. Nicole and Rashawn leapt to their feet to help him, and after what seemed like forever, they managed to shut the door, getting themselves drenched once again.

"What happened?" Nicole asked.

"The four-wheeler must be buried under debris," Chase answered. "Or maybe it floated away. The balloon tires could have lifted it like a boat in the current."

"What do you mean by the current?" Rashawn asked.

"There's a lot of water out there. The surge. Flooding. Right now, the only thing keeping the water out of the barn — or most of the water anyway — is the debris. It's formed a dam."

"What are we going to do?" Nicole asked.

"I guess I'm going to have to make my way to the Shop after all."

"I'll go with you," Nicole said.

"There's no point in that. It won't take two of us to bring back a can of gas."

"What's it like out there?" Rashawn asked.

"Not too bad," Chase lied.

John Masters crawled on his stomach, playing out the steel cable from the power winch bolted to the front of Tomás's truck, which was still precariously balanced on its side on the old railroad bridge. Cindy and Mark had crept ahead to the end of the trestle and were crouched behind an uprooted tree in a futile attempt to stay out of the vicious wind. The only person who was out of the wind was Tomás. He was behind the steering wheel, waiting for his partner to right the truck. Engines were not designed to operate sideways. Someone had to stay in the cab and play with the accelerator to keep the engine idling. John had once again offered to spell him from behind the wheel, and once again Tomás had refused, adding in Spanglish that he would be grateful if John could get the truck to tip onto the tracks rather than into the swamp.

John was doing his best. The water was rising quickly. It had almost reached the bottom of the ties. John hoped he had the cable angles figured correctly. He fished the hook under the second rail, attached it back onto the cable, then crawled back to the truck and spoke to Tomás through the smashed windshield.

"You ready, amigo?"

"Minute," Tomás said. He pulled the last two photographs of his family off the dash and put them with the others in a Ziploc bag. "*Sí.* Ready."

"When I get it righted, drive forward just enough to loosen the slack. I'll spool the cable and jump in the cab."

"*Vaya con Dios,*" Tomás said.

"*Gracias,*" John replied.

He started the winch.

"Are you sure the camera's safe?" Mark asked.

"Strapped in like a toddler," Cindy answered as she watched John's headlamp bobbing around the tracks in the dark and the two truck headlights vertical rather than horizontal.

"You really think we can make a living going freelance?"

"You mean if we live through this storm?"

"Right."

"Well, it won't be easy, but I think we can make a living . . . eventually."

"And you think John Masters is a worthy subject of a documentary?"

"Maybe," Cindy said. "We'll have to see how the story develops. You have to admit that it's been pretty dramatic so far."

"I've never been more scared in my life," Mark said. "If that's what you mean."

"Me too," Cindy admitted. "I don't think I would have tagged along if I'd known how bad this hurricane was going to be, yet John and Tomás don't appear the least bit worried."

"That's because they are insane," Mark said.

"You've got a point, but they have managed to keep us alive."

"So far," Mark said. "But if we don't get out of here soon, we'll be swimming to the highway. Did I mention that I can't swim?"

"A few dozen times. Look!" Cindy said. "The headlights are horizontal."

"Yeah," Mark said. "But are they right side up?"

John Masters let out a sigh of relief as Tomás drove the truck forward to give him enough slack to unhook the cable. He spooled it up and climbed into the cab. Inside, Tomás was reattaching his family to the dash.

"You can't go out there alone," Nicole insisted.

She had followed Chase to the door at the far end of the barn.

"Believe me," Chase said, "I don't want to go out there whether it's with you or without you, but I don't see any other choice. You and Momma Rossi said there could be a problem if Pet has her calf in the dark."

"A two-hundred-and-twenty-five-pound problem," Nicole said.

"That's how much a baby elephant weighs when it's born?"

"Give or take a few pounds."

"We need light," Chase said.

"Let me get the gas," Nicole said. "I know the farm a lot better than you do."

"But you don't know the Shop."

"Back to my original argument," Nicole said. "We should both go."

Chase didn't like it, but Nicole had a good point. He'd only been on the Rossi farm a day before the hurricane struck. He was certain he could find the building where they had parked their rigs, but if he ran into trouble getting there, or getting back, Nicole would have a better idea about how to get around the problem.

"And there's Hector," Nicole added.

Chase had forgotten about Hector, or perhaps he had intentionally put him out of his mind. Having an aggressive leopard running loose was something he didn't want to think about.

"What are the chances of running into him?" Chase asked.

Nicole shrugged her shoulders. "Hard to say. With luck he might be hunkered down somewhere waiting the storm out."

"And eating Poco," Chase added.

"Unfortunately, that meal is probably long over."

"What could you do that I couldn't do if I was unlucky enough to run into Hector?" Chase asked.

"Hector is not the only reason I want to go with you," Nicole said. "I need to check on the other animals. If Hector's out, there's a good chance other animals are loose too."

Suddenly, sitting in a dark barn with a pregnant elephant seemed a lot more attractive to Chase. "What are the chances of Pet having her calf in the next few hours?"

"Good, according to Momma Rossi," Nicole answered. "And she thinks there's a very good chance that Pet isn't going to take care of her calf. These are not ideal circumstances to have your first baby. If there's a problem, we'll have to catch the calf and take it away so it doesn't get stepped on."

"Hard to do in the dark," Chase said.

"Hard to do in the *light*," Nicole pointed out. "Wait here."

"Where are you going?"

"I have to get something from the bunkhouse." She hurried away.

While he waited, Chase slowly turned the door handle, expecting the door to fly open and hit him in the face. It didn't. Cautiously he peered out into the darkness with his headlamp, and was pleased to see the downwind side was calm compared to the opposite end of the circus barn. They wouldn't have to worry about WPPs until they stepped out from the shelter of the wall. There was a lot of water buildup to his left — the same direction they'd have to travel to reach the barn where the Shack & Shop was parked. Between the Shack & Shop and the circus barn were two other barns, one of which was the barn where Hector *used* to live. Chase's father had taught him hundreds of survival techniques over the past couple of years, but how to survive a leopard attack was not one of them.

Chase slowly scanned the windblown darkness with his headlamp, hoping to see the four-wheeler with its precious load of fuel. There was no sign of it. He was kicking himself for not having had the sense to put it inside the barn when he felt a tap on his shoulder. He ducked back inside and closed the door.

"How is it out there?" Nicole asked.

"Not as bad as it is on the other end," Chase answered as he shook the rain out of his hair. "I should have at least tied the four-wheeler down. There was plenty of time before the wind started up again after the eye."

"You couldn't have known that it would be buried or blown away," Nicole said.

"I should have known." He turned and looked at her. "Is that a —"

"Shotgun," Nicole said. "With twelve-gauge double-ought shells. Just in case."

"In case of what?"

"In case of Hector."

"Do you know how to use that thing?"

Nicole pumped a shell into the breech. "Yes, I do, but I hope I don't have to use it." She reached behind her back and pulled out a pistol. "If we run into Hector, I'd prefer to use this, but he may not give us a chance. It's a tranquilizer pistol. I think it'll fit into one of your cargo pockets. The safety's on. It won't go off."

"I'm glad to hear that." Chase put the pistol in his pocket.

"Momma Rossi won't want me to go," Nicole said. "So I'm not going to tell her until just before we head out."

"I don't want you to go either," Chase said.

"I'm going. Ready?"

Chase turned the handle.

"I'm going with Chase to get gas," Nicole shouted over her shoulder as they stepped out into Hurricane Emily.

"Big surprise," Momma Rossi said after the door closed.

"I knew she was going too," Rashawn said.

Momma Rossi fixed her dark eyes on Rashawn. "Now that we're alone, tell me what you and Nicole and Chase are keeping from me."

Reluctantly, Rashawn told her about Poco and Hector.

"Poor little Poco," Momma Rossi said. "I didn't see that coming."

"I'm sorry about your monkey," Rashawn said.

"Exactly where did you see Hector?"

"I can't say *exactly* because I've never been here before, but it wasn't far from the gate we came through. He was headed the same way we were going, but we were faster on the four-wheeler."

"He was probably looking for shelter just like you were," Momma Rossi said.

"What did you mean by you didn't *see* that coming?" Rashawn asked.

"My mother and her mother had second sight, and it was passed on to me," Momma Rossi answered. "Their sight was much clearer than mine."

"So, you're a psychic?"

Momma Rossi smiled. "Part-time, and I'm afraid I'm not very talented at it."

"Chase said that you knew Hurricane Emily was going to get your house."

"*Knew* is too strong of a word. If I had *known*, I wouldn't have been inside the house when the wind started to take it apart. I would have put Poco in a crate so he couldn't have run out the front door when we escaped. I would have known that Hector was on the loose."

05:52 AM

"Stay next to the wall!" Chase shouted. "I'll lead us to the edge of the building, then you can take over."

The barn protected them from the brunt of the savage wind, but it was still strong enough to knock them down if they weren't careful.

"There's a lot of water," Nicole said.

"I know. I'm worried about it." It looked like the barn was on the bank of a flooding river. Chase bent closer to Nicole. "The only higher ground than this is where your house is — or was. What's behind the house?"

"Woods," Nicole answered. "And a lake."

Chase hadn't seen the lake the day before. That explained where the water was coming from. "How big is it?"

"Big. But it's never overflowed before, and our family has lived here for seventy years."

It's flooding now, Chase thought. *Big-time.* He visualized the lay of the land, thinking back to the tour Nicole had given him upon his arrival just two days earlier. The road to the farm was below them, which meant that it was probably swamped with water running down to the other lake, where their school bus had sunk. His father and Tomás were not going to have an easy time getting to the farm.

Chase and Nicole inched their way along the wall to where Chase hoped they'd find the four-wheeler around the corner of the building. What they found instead was a dead giraffe.

"Gertrude!" Nicole shouted above the howling wind.

Chase had seen a lot of bad things the past couple years, but the dead giraffe was the worst. There was something terribly wrong with the sight of a fourteen-foot giraffe lying on the ground with floodwater sluicing around it.

Nicole waded out and put her arms around Gertrude's long neck, totally ignoring the wind and flying debris. Hesitantly, Chase joined her. He felt bad about Gertrude, but now was not the time for either of them to pay their last respects. He needed to get Nicole out of there.

"I'm sorry about Gertrude," Chase said. "But we can't stay here. We have to move."

He glanced to his left just in time to see the farmhouse's heavy front door and frame cartwheeling its way directly at them. He grabbed Nicole by the arm and yanked her to the side. The door clipped one of Gertrude's front legs, snapping it like a brittle branch, then sailed off into the night.

"That was close." Nicole shuddered. "Thank you."

"No problem. Now let's get out of here before the next WPP comes barreling down this wind tunnel."

"Gertrude's still warm. She couldn't have been dead very long."

"Can we talk about Gertrude once we get inside the next building?"

"Sorry."

They didn't get very far. Halfway to the second building, they came across a lion. It was not dead.

05:53 AM

"I vote for going to the shelter," Mark said. "At least long enough to get some coffee and use the bathroom."

"It *would* give us a chance to check up on the latest hurricane reports," Cindy added.

John hated to backtrack, but he had to agree: Going to the emergency shelter was probably their best option at the moment. They needed to check the truck out. Something was wrong with the steering. Tomás was having a difficult time keeping the 4x4 on the highway, and it wasn't just because of Hurricane Emily.

A police cruiser with flashing lights marked the road to the emergency shelter. The policeman stayed inside his car, waving them past with a flashlight. The road led them to a large high school gymnasium. The parking lot looked as if the state basketball tournament were being played.

"A lot of people didn't make it home," Cindy said.

Mark pointed. "There's a parking spot."

Tomás drove by the empty spot, then passed up three more.

"Where are you going?" Cindy asked.

Tomás didn't answer.

John switched on a spotlight outside the passenger window. "Before we go inside we need to circle the building and check for structural damage."

"The gym's made out of concrete," Mark pointed out.

"Water can take down any building regardless of the material," John said. "Water's the most powerful thing on earth. The Grand Canyon was created by water." He swung the spotlight between the foundation and the roofline as they slowly circled the building. When they got back to the parking lot he switched the spot off.

"Well?" Mark asked.

"So far so good," John answered. "Hope you brought rubber boots."

"I can't remember the last time I was dry," Mark said.

Tomás parked the truck, jumped out, then disappeared from sight.

"Where'd he go?" Cindy asked.

"Under the truck. Something's broken. Why don't you and Mark head into the gym? Tomás and I will be in after we figure out the problem. Watch out for WPPs. And when you get inside find a spot near one of the exits to hang out. You'll want to be near a door if the building starts to collapse."

"Good safety tip," Mark said.

He and Cindy waded through the ankle-deep water to the gymnasium.

05:56 AM

"Don't move," Nicole said.

Chase wasn't sure if she was talking to him or to the lion, but he froze in midstep just to be safe.

Nicole put her lips close to his ear and whispered, "It's Simba. He can't see us." Her warm breath sent a shiver down his neck, or maybe it was the lion's unblinking eyes drilling into him. "Our headlamps are blinding him," Nicole continued. "We're downwind, so he can't smell us either. And he can't hear us with the wind rattling the metal buildings. He's as confused and frightened as we are."

Simba was standing fifteen feet away and did not look confused or frightened to Chase. He looked hungry and impossibly big. Nicole had told him the day before that Simba had been retired from the circus after mauling his trainer. If Simba was loose, the other lions might be loose as well. Three females and one immature male. Simba was twice as big as the young male. Right now, he looked like he was ready to pounce and tear them to shreds.

"On the count of three we'll turn our headlamps off," Nicole whispered. "While Simba's eyes adjust back to the dark, he'll be temporarily blinded and we'll run over to the next building."

Temporarily blinded? Chase thought. *How long does* temporary *last?*

Nicole was cradling the shotgun in her arms, which seemed like a better, and more permanent, solution to their lion problem than turning their headlamps off.

". . . three," Nicole said.

What happened to one and two?

Chase switched his headlamp off a second behind Nicole. She grabbed his arm and pulled him to the left. Simba might have been temporarily blinded, but so were they. Chase couldn't see a thing. He allowed Nicole to drag him into the darkness.

They got to the wall of the second building and started inching along it with the wind at their backs. Chase hoped there weren't four lions in front of them.

06:00 AM

"What are you two doing here?" Richard Krupp shouted across the crowded gymnasium.

Cindy and Mark had not even checked in with the emergency worker at the table near the entrance when Richard Krupp, the number one news anchor in Saint Petersburg, Florida, barreled his way to the front of the line.

"We're here for the basketball game," Mark said. "The weather slowed us down a bit. Who's winning?"

"I'm serious," Richard said.

"So am I." Mark glanced at the emblem on the wall of the dimly lit gym. "I never miss a Florida Hams game."

"I think it says *Rams*," Cindy said.

"Whatever. I never miss one of their games. Hey! What's with all the cots on the court?"

Cindy laughed.

Richard glowered. "You won't be cracking jokes in a couple hours when you get fired for not showing up for work."

"No worries," Mark said. "We resigned."

"Really."

"Yep."

"When?"

"A couple hours ago. We dropped by to let you know."

"I thought you said you came here for a basketball game."

"That too."

"Why'd you quit?"

"We had an epiphany."

"That's a big word, Mark."

"It was a big feeling, Richard."

"How'd you get here?"

"Drove."

"Station vehicle?"

"Private vehicle."

"But you still have the station camera. Give it to me and I'll take it back."

"No can do, Richard. I signed my life away for this thing. I'll return it personally."

"What about the video inside?"

"That too."

"I can take it from you."

"You can try." Mark smiled.

"Back off, both of you," Cindy said. "We're wet, we're tired, and we're hungry." She looked at Richard. "And we are not giving you the video we shot."

Richard Krupp backed off, but not very far. He pulled his sat phone out and woke the station manager from a very sound sleep.

The walk to the end of the second barn seemed to take an hour, but according to Chase's watch it was less than five minutes. The luminous hands looked as bright as the sun in the pitch dark.

If I can see the hands, Simba can see the hands.

Chase slipped the watch off his wrist and stuffed it into his pocket, next to the tranquilizer gun.

He and Nicole found the door to the barn open, banging against the metal side. Chase went over the list of animals Nicole had shown him during his tour of the barn.

One brown bear. Three zebras. Four ostriches. Some parrots. And Hector . . .

Nicole started to go in, but Chase put his hand on her shoulder. "What are the chances of Hector sneaking back inside here to get away from the hurricane?"

Nicole stopped and frowned.

"So there is a chance that we are standing between a lion and a leopard," Chase continued. "Is there any gas inside the barn?"

Nicole shook her head.

"Maybe we should skip inspecting this barn and go directly to the barn where the Shack and Shop is parked. We don't have a lot of time before the generator runs dry."

"I need to check on the animals," Nicole said. "If I'd checked earlier, Gertrude might still be alive."

"What could you have done?"

"That's the problem," Nicole said. "I'll never know."

"We also don't *know* if Hector is inside here waiting for us. The door's wide open. Simba might be waiting inside for us as well."

"I doubt Simba slipped in front of us."

"No problem, then," Chase said. "We'll just walk into a dark barn with a bear, a few zebras, some ostriches and parrots, and maybe a killer leopard."

"I get your point," Nicole said with a slight smile. "It's not a smart move. Why don't you go get the gas and pick me up on your way back?"

"No. We're sticking together."

"Well, then *we* need to check on the animals."

Chase knew there was no point in arguing with her further, and they were wasting time.

"I'll go in first," Nicole said.

"Be my guest. You're the one with the shotgun."

Nicole took two steps into the barn and stopped. Chase followed and closed the door firmly so Simba couldn't sneak in behind them.

Providing he isn't already in the barn waiting to devour us.

Chase looked around nervously, slicing his headlamp back

and forth through the darkness. Any second, he expected Hector to attack, or the bear to run out of the shadows and tear his head off.

They stepped deeper into the darkness. Chase glanced down to see two inches of standing water covering the cement floor.

"How far are we from the coast?" Chase asked.

"What?"

"The surge," Chase said. "This water isn't just coming from the lake in back of your house. There's too much of it. I think we're getting floodwaters from two directions."

"The gulf is three miles away as the crow flies," Nicole said. "Maybe a little less."

She took a few more tentative steps forward. Something moved to their left. Something big.

"Bear," Nicole said.

Chase swung his headlamp in the direction of the movement. The bear was twenty feet away from them, pushing on the metal wall with his giant paw.

"We'll be okay," Nicole said calmly.

"I guess that depends on your definition of *okay*," Chase said.

06:07 AM

John and Tomás stepped into the gymnasium.

Organized, John thought. *And relatively calm. Probably about two hundred people.* He had been in a dozen shelters over the past two years, in gymnasiums, sports arenas, and convention centers. When he and Tomás had first started following weather disasters, they had gone to shelters to solicit work but quickly learned that most of the people in shelters had nowhere else to go. Business owners and wealthy people stayed on their properties, checked into high-end hotels, or left town altogether.

John and Tomás had entered the gym near the makeshift hospital area, where people were being treated for all sorts of weather injuries: lacerations, bruises, broken bones, heart attacks, nervous breakdowns. . . . Nurses and doctors scurried between cots treating wounds, checking IV fluids, replacing ice packs, and handing out medications.

A food and water station had been set up in the middle of the gym so everyone could get to it easily. It was crowded with people grabbing donuts, pizza, water, and coffee.

Breakfast of champions.

Surrounding the station was a sea of cots and folding chairs filled with people wondering how long it would be before they could go home, assuming they still had homes. At their feet were boxes and bags of precious possessions they could not leave behind.

"Name, address, social security number," the emergency worker said, sliding two clipboards to them. "I'll need to see some identification too if you have it."

Their IDs were wet. They flipped open their swollen wallets and filled out the forms.

The emergency worker looked at the licenses. "Whoa, a long way from home. What brings you to this neck of the woods?"

"Just passing through," John said.

"Bad timing."

"Tell me about it."

"Are either of you injured?"

"No. Just tired and wet."

"The locker room is open if you don't mind a cold shower. We're using generators for the lights and heat. Not enough juice to warm the water, but you'll find plenty of towels. I'm afraid there are no dry clothes. We brought in a big load, but they were all used up by the first wave."

"We'll be fine." John scanned the gym for Cindy and Mark, but he didn't see them.

"What's it like out there?" the emergency worker asked, as John and Tomás headed toward the locker room.

"Breezy," John said. "Wet."

06:09 AM

"Brutus," Nicole said. "He's been on the farm longer than I have."

"Has he ever mauled anyone?" Chase asked.

"No," Nicole answered. "I'm not saying that we should walk up and scratch his belly, but he's not aggressive."

"He's not in his cage either."

"Brutus is more afraid of us than we are of him."

"Speak for yourself."

Brutus didn't look the least bit afraid. He had managed to loosen the corner of one of the metal panels and was trying to tear it off the wall.

Why didn't he just walk through the open door? Chase thought. *Maybe Brutus isn't as bright as he is big.*

"Do you think he'll get that panel off?" Nicole asked.

Chase shook his head. "The panels are attached with long bolts screwed into treated posts. For the time being he's not going anywhere unless he knows how to open a door, which reminds me . . . Who opened the door?"

"I've been thinking about that. It had to be Hector."

"How does a leopard open a door?"

"It's a bar handle on the inside. All he'd have to do is jump up and give it a swipe with his paw."

"Lucky swipe," Chase said.

"Maybe not."

"What do you mean?"

"Hector is smarter than your average cat. He's a watcher. He's seen me come in and out through that door hundreds of times. I think he's been waiting for the opportunity."

Chase shined his headlamp at Hector's cage. The door was closed, but the chain-link fencing was hanging down. "How'd that happen?"

Nicole pointed at the bear cage. The door was gone. "I'd say that Brutus managed to tear his door off. Probably in a panic from the sound of the wind. He must have torn into the chain link on Hector's cage."

Chase glanced back at the door they'd walked through. "You think Hector's figured out how to open it from the outside?"

Nicole shook her head. "It's a twist knob on the outside. As long as Hector isn't in here, we're safe."

"Except for the bear," Chase said.

06:12 AM

Rashawn broke off a flake of hay and threw it to the elephant. Pet picked the flake up with her trunk and tossed it over her back.

"Guess she's not hungry," Rashawn said.

Momma Rossi smiled. "She's been off her feed for days. We're just giving her food to keep her mind off her discomfort and the wind."

Pet yanked on the chains around her left front ankle and right rear ankle.

"Doesn't look like it's working," Rashawn said.

A far-off look clouded Momma Rossi's face.

"What's wrong?" Rashawn asked.

Momma Rossi didn't answer. Her distant expression deepened.

"Momma Rossi?"

Rashawn glanced over at Pet. The elephant was standing perfectly still for the first time since they'd stepped into the barn. She was staring at Momma Rossi as if she could see right through her.

"Are you okay, Momma Rossi?" Rashawn tried to stay calm, hoping the old woman wasn't having a stroke or something. "Can you hear me? Is anyone home? Earth to Momma —"

Momma Rossi blinked, then sighed, and said, "That was a strong one."

She looked a little wobbly, almost as if she might collapse. Rashawn rushed forward and took her arm. "Is it your heart?"

"Oh no, dear. It wasn't my heart. It was a . . . Well, for lack of a better word, a premonition."

"You mean you had a vision?"

"*Vision* is too clear of a word. It's more like a flash of insight."

"What did you see?"

"It's too early to tell. It takes awhile for my old brain to catch up with the sight and define it."

"Are Chase and Nicole all right?"

"I think I'd know if they weren't. I didn't get the sense that they were in trouble. At least at this moment."

"What's that mean?"

"I'm not sure. I have a feeling that things are going to get worse before they get better. Much worse."

"Did you get any . . . uh . . . vibes about your son?"

"Marco?" Momma Rossi closed her eyes for a few seconds, then opened them again. "Nothing."

Rashawn took a deep breath. "What about my family?"

"Give me your hand."

Rashawn placed her hand in Momma Rossi's tiny one. The old woman fixed her dark eyes on Rashawn's for a full minute before saying anything.

"They are in a kitchen. All three of them. Your mother is asleep in a green leather chair with her feet up. She's holding a young boy in her lap."

"That's my daddy's green recliner! They must have dragged it into the kitchen from the living room. My momma and little brother nap in it all the time. What was my daddy doing?"

"Playing cards at a table."

"Solitaire! He always plays when he's stressed or thinking about something."

"I can't pick up people's thoughts," Momma Rossi said. "But I bet he's worrying about you."

"I bet he is too," Rashawn said. "It's kind of weird that you can see our kitchen without ever having been in it." She took her hand away. "But I'm glad they're okay."

"I'm glad too," Momma Rossi said. "Do you think your rice trick has fixed the phone?"

"Only one way to find out." Rashawn took the satellite phone out of the plastic bag and snapped in the battery. "Here goes nothing."

She pressed the button. The orange display came on.

"No signal," Rashawn said. "I don't know much about these things. I wonder if you have to point them at the sky for them to work."

She walked over to the small window by Pet's ring, holding the phone out in front of her.

"Two bars! Now if we only had someone to call. My daddy just has a regular cell phone, and no one's been able to get a cell signal since yesterday."

"The cell towers were probably damaged because of Emily," Momma Rossi pointed out.

"Maybe I can hit the redial button and get ahold of Chase's dad," Rashawn said.

She didn't have to. The satellite phone rang.

06:19 AM

"What time is it?"

"Ummm . . . I don't know," Rashawn said slowly. "I don't wear a watch."

"Sorry . . . uh . . . that's a game that Chase and I play. Is this Nicole?"

"Rashawn."

"Hi, Rashawn. This is John Masters. Can I speak to Chase?"

"He's not here."

"Where is he?"

"Out trying to find gas for the generator."

"You mean *outside*?"

"Yes, sir, with Nicole."

"It's going to be light soon, and it's not that cold. Why did he go outside in the middle of a hurricane to get gas?"

"Sun's not going to shine where we are even after it comes up."

"Are you in the basement of the Rossis' house?"

"We're in the barn. There *is* no house. Emily turned it into sticks."

"Which barn are you in?"

"The one with Pet."

"Pet?"

"The elephant."

"Did you say *elephant*?"

"Yeah, you know . . . the one that's pregnant. She's supposed to have her baby any moment now. Be bad if she had it in the pitch dark. If there was a problem, we wouldn't be able to get the baby away from her. The wind has Pet all agitated, as you can probably imagine," Rashawn concluded matter-of-factly.

"It's hard to imagine any of this. I didn't know the Rossis had an elephant on their farm."

"It's a circus."

"Sounds like it. Is Marco there?"

"No, sir. We don't know where he is, and Nicole is sick over it. Chase said you might be able to find him."

"I can try. Do you know what kind of vehicle he's driving?"

"Just a minute . . . White Chevy Tahoe."

"What's the condition of the building you're in?"

"It's holding up, but the wind is slamming into the sides. There's water coming in on one end."

"The windward side?"

"I guess."

"How much water?"

"There's six inches on the cement. Maybe a little more, but most of the barn is dry."

"What's your backup shelter?"

Rashawn hesitated. "What do you mean?"

"Where are you going to go if the building you're in starts to collapse?"

"I don't know."

"I'm sure Chase has thought of a backup."

"I'm sure he has. He's like some kind of storm superhero. He knows exactly what to do . . . well, most of the time he does. None of us knows what to do about Hector."

"Who's Hector?"

"The leopard."

"As in big cat?"

"Big enough. And he killed Poco."

"Slow down, Rashawn. Who's Poco?"

"Momma Rossi's monkey."

"Momma Rossi?"

"You don't know much about the farm, do you?"

"Apparently not."

"Momma Rossi is Marco's mom."

"And she has a monkey?"

"She *had* a monkey until Hector killed it."

"Is Momma Rossi there?"

"She's standing right here. You want to talk to her?"

"I guess I'd better, but before you hand the phone over to her, check the battery level."

"Hang on. . . . It's in the red."

"I was afraid of that. There's a charger and spare battery in Chase's go bag."

"You mean his backpack?"

"Right."

"He dumped it after our school bus sank. He stuffed some things in those big pockets he has on his pants, but I don't know what they were."

"How long has he been gone?"

"I can't say exactly. Maybe a half an hour. This is my first time on this farm. Chase said something about a shack and a shop? I don't know how far they are from here."

"It can't be far. You be careful, Rashawn. Let me talk to Mrs. Rossi."

"You be careful too, Mr. Masters. Nice talking to you."

A terrible scream rose above the clattering wind. Chase's knees nearly buckled at the sound.

"What — ?"

"Sulfur-crested cockatoo," Nicole said. "Nothing to worry — watch out!" She tackled Chase. A charging ostrich missed them by inches, then hit the wall behind them with a loud bang.

Nicole was up on her feet and running back to the door before Chase could piece together what had happened. He checked on Brutus, making sure the bear was still worrying the metal panel, before getting to his feet and following her.

The two-hundred-pound ostrich was thrashing on the cement floor, trying to get up, which was not going to happen with two broken legs.

"I hate this hurricane!" Nicole shouted bitterly as she dodged the bird's flailing feet.

With tears running down her face, she pointed the shotgun at the ostrich's head and pulled the trigger. The bird continued to thrash for several seconds, then stopped. Nicole walked outside.

Chase found her leaning against the wall, sobbing. The shotgun was on the ground at her feet. He picked it up and waited.

Nicole wiped her tears on her sleeve. "You were right," she said.

"About what?"

"About the animals. There's nothing we can do to help them in the dark. We need to get the gas and go back to the circus barn. The only animal we can help at this point is Pet."

"Why don't you go back to the barn?" Chase said. "I can get the gas on my own."

Nicole took the shotgun. She ejected the spent shell and jacked a fresh one into the breech. "Not with Simba and Hector running around, you can't. And who knows what else has escaped. We have four other lions besides Simba, you know."

"Yeah, I know," Chase said. "You think they're out too?"

"They were in the same barn as Simba."

Just the mention of Simba's name sent a chill down Chase's back.

"Gertrude — the giraffe — she was in that barn too," Nicole continued. "At fourteen feet, the only way she could have gotten out is if the big door was open."

"Or if the building collapsed," Chase added. He looked up at the sky. "Eventually the storm's going to pass. I think the winds have already died down."

The diving board from the Rossis' swimming pool tumbled

through the open area before them and disappeared into the dark.

Nicole grinned. "You were saying?"

"I didn't say the winds had stopped," Chase said. "What do you usually do with escaped man-eaters?"

"They aren't man-eaters, but they are potentially dangerous. We've had a few escapes inside the barn, but they've never gotten outside the barn. The important thing now is containment."

"We're way past containment." Chase looked out at the Rossis' land. "We're in out-of-control."

06:24 AM

John found Cindy and Mark sitting on a cot with towels around their necks, drinking coffee and eating donuts. Mark had the precious TV station camera in his lap.

"How's the truck?" Mark asked.

"Beyond our ability to repair without new parts. We were lucky to have gotten this far."

"Did you try to reach Chase again?" Cindy asked.

John nodded. "His phone's working, but he didn't answer. A girl picked up, Rashawn. She was on the bus with them. I spoke to Marco's mother too, but only for a minute or two. The phone battery was going dead, but it sounds like there are some other problems on the farm."

John went on to explain what Rashawn and Mrs. Rossi had told him. Cindy and Mark stared at him in complete silence.

Mark shook his head. "I'm sorry," he said slowly. "I don't understand. You mean like an African leopard, spotted, with fangs and claws?"

"It could be an Asian leopard," Cindy said. "They have them too, although not as many as they have in Africa."

Mark looked at Cindy. "Thanks, Mother Nature." He turned to John. "There's a leopard running around this farm your son is on, and it's carrying a dead monkey in its mouth?"

"That's right."

"And your son is running around looking for gas so that the elephant that lives on this so-called farm doesn't have to give birth in the dark?"

John nodded. "That about sums it up. Except Marco was out looking for the kids and didn't make it back home. I promised his mother I'd try to find him."

"Does he know that he doesn't have a home?" Cindy asked.

"I doubt it. Mrs. Rossi said he left before the wind took it down. She barely made it out herself before it collapsed. I have to get back to the farm. Tomás is trying to find someone to lend us a vehicle."

"You really think someone is going to give you their wheels to drive around in a hurricane?" Mark asked.

"We'll pay them of course," John said.

"Pay for what?" Richard Krupp appeared as if out of nowhere. "Aren't you that construction guy Cindy was interviewing on my news show?"

John turned to the news anchor. He was shorter and thinner than he looked on television. "I'm that guy," he said.

"Did you drive Cindy and Mark here?"

"My partner Tomás and I did."

"Why?"

"We were headed in the same direction. How did *you* get here?"

"A television van. We would have made it all the way to Palm Breeze if we hadn't been turned back at the roadblock. I live in Palm Breeze. My wife's the principal of Palm Breeze Middle School."

Cindy rolled her eyes. "What do you want now, Richard?"

"The video you shot on the way here, for one." Richard looked at Mark. "And the camera on your lap. I just got off the phone with your boss."

"He's your boss too," Mark said.

"Whatever. He was surprised to hear you two had quit, but he wasn't upset. He already has people in mind to take your places. I think his exact words were: 'No big deal. There's a dynamite reporter up in Tallahassee who wants to come south. And cameramen are a dime a dozen.'"

"Ouch," Mark said.

"He also told me to get the camera and video. And before you say no, I've talked with the police here at the shelter." Richard tilted his head. Two uniformed police officers stood twenty feet behind him, staring at them. "They'd be happy to take the camera away from you if you want to play it that way."

"We haven't officially resigned yet," Cindy said.

"Doesn't matter. The station wants the camera and video until you work this out *officially*. Can't blame them. The camera is worth a lot of money."

Cindy looked at her watch. "Technically we aren't even late for work . . . yet."

"Technically you've violated policy by using station equipment without authorization. Listen, we can do it the easy way or the hard way. It's up to you."

The officers took a step forward as if on cue.

"Can we borrow your television van?" John asked.

"What?" Richard said.

"We need it," John said. "Our vehicle is out of commission."

Richard smiled at Cindy and Mark. "Lucky you two made it this far safely. Your driver's nuts."

John returned the smile. "Didn't you say your wife is the principal at Palm Breeze Middle School?"

"What does that have to do with your needing my news van?"

John glanced at the officers, then lowered his voice. "You might want to have your guys back off before I answer that question. And don't worry, Mark isn't going to run out into Hurricane Emily with your camera."

Richard thought about it for a second, then turned around and held up his hand to keep the officers at bay. "What's this all about?" he asked quietly. "And make it quick. I have to do a stand-up for the morning news in a few minutes."

"When's the last time you talked to your wife?" John asked.

"Yesterday afternoon just before school got out. She was checking on Hurricane Emily. Why?"

"Where did you tell her Emily was going to hit?"

"Saint Pete. That's where we thought it was going to land at the time. Then the power went out, and we lost cell service, and I was unable to reach her. What does this have to do with —"

"She put the kids on the bus," John interrupted.

"*Two* buses," Richard said. "Most of the kids at the school were picked up and driven home by their parents, or driven out of town ahead of the storm."

"Well, *one* bus didn't make it," John said. "It sank in a lake with three kids and the bus driver."

Richard turned pale. "I didn't hear anything about this, and we've been monitoring police and emergency bands all night. How do you know?"

"Because my son was one of the three kids on that bus when it sank. Your wife should have never put them on that bus, but she's not the one I blame. Her husband, the number one news anchor in Saint Pete, told her the hurricane of the century was not going to hit Palm Breeze."

"Is your son okay?"

"He didn't drown, if that's what you mean, but the driver did."

"The driver's dead?"

John nodded.

Richard gave a cheery wave to the police officers. "We're good here," he said. "Everything is resolved. It was just a misunderstanding. Thanks."

The two officers shrugged and walked away. Richard sat down on the edge of the cot. "Are the kids here?"

"No. Chase and the two girls made their way from the lake to the Rossi farm."

"The circus Rossis?"

"You know them?"

"Palm Breeze isn't that big," Richard said. "And the Rossis are kind of . . . well, unusual. Have you told Marco?"

"No. I talked to one of the girls and Marco's mother on my sat phone. Their house is gone."

Richard shook his head. "So, where are they now?"

"Holed up in a barn with a pregnant elephant and a leopard on the loose," Cindy said.

"We did a report on that cat," Richard said slowly. "Animal control wanted to euthanize it, but Marco stepped in and said he would take it. That's one dangerous creature on the loose."

"I'm aware of that," John said. "Listen, I know that you and your wife didn't mean to cause any harm, but you both made a terrible mistake. A man's dead. We need to get to the Rossis' before anyone else gets killed or injured, and we need your van to do it."

"All right," Richard said. "But my crew and I are going with you."

Cindy shook her head. "Sorry, Richard. No room. This is Mark's and my story. After what we've gone through, we're not about to give it to you. With John, Tomás, and the two of us that's almost a full boat."

"There's room in the van for one more, and it's my van," Richard said quietly. "I'm going with you."

John shrugged.

"The roadblocks are still up," Richard said. "They aren't even letting FEMA through. Do you have any idea how you're going to get to the Rossis' farm?"

"I know where *not* to go," John said.

"We should ask Marco," Richard said. "The Rossis have been in this area for decades. At one time they owned a big chunk of the county."

"If we could get him on the phone, I would," John said.

Richard looked confused. "I guess you didn't understand when I asked if you had *told* Marco. He's here."

"At the shelter?"

"I saw him twenty minutes ago on the far side of the gym carrying a bottle of water and a slice of pizza. I didn't talk to him, but it was definitely Marco. The Rossis are the only little people around here. I assumed he was here with his whole family."

"I'll find him," John said, starting across the gym.

"I guess I'd better tell my crew there's been a change of plans," Richard said, and walked off.

"Was Richard actually acting like a human being for a second?" Mark asked.

"Surprised me too," Cindy said.

"Does this mean we still have jobs?"

"It might," Cindy answered. "But I'm not feeling like much of a reporter at the moment. I can't believe I didn't put together the connection between Richard's wife and Chase's school bus."

"You got bested by a builder."

"I told you there was more to John Masters than meets the eye."

"I still think he's a little crazy."

"You probably would be too if you'd been struck by lightning."

06:33 AM

The sat phone rang. Rashawn rushed over to grab it from the windowsill and answered it before the second ring. Momma Rossi was curled up, asleep on two bales of hay Rashawn had dragged over from the stack.

"Hello?" she said quietly.

"John Masters. Rashawn?"

"Yes, sir."

"Can I speak to Mrs. Rossi?"

"She's taking a nap, but I can wake her."

"Hang on. . . . Marco says to let her sleep."

"You found Mr. Rossi?"

"He's standing right next to me and he's fine."

Rashawn smiled. "Nicole will be so relieved! I just hope my family is okay too. I haven't heard from them since this whole thing started."

"What's your last name? We're at a shelter. We can check to see if they're here."

"I think they're home," Rashawn said, recalling Momma Rossi's vision. "But it would be good if you could check. Our last name is Stone."

John said something to someone, then got back on the line. "Are Chase and Nicole back?"

Rashawn's smile faded. "Not yet. And I'm worried."

"Moving around in this kind of weather is not like moving around in regular weather."

"I know. It took us nearly twelve hours to go five miles last night, but I'm still worried."

"Hang on a second," John said. After a moment he got back on. "Your family's not here. So you're probably right. They're at home riding the storm out."

"I hope so," Rashawn said.

"How's the barn holding up?"

"It's in one piece, but there's still water coming in on the one side I told you about."

"No structural damage?"

"Nothing I can see."

"Remind Chase to check the barn out when he comes back. He'll know what to look for."

"I'm sure he will. Before they left he went over the barn with a fine-tooth comb."

"We're going to try to get to you. I'm not sure if we'll succeed, but we'll give it our best shot."

"That's all anyone can do," Rashawn said. "Don't kill yourself trying to get here. That won't do anyone any good."

John laughed.

"What's so funny?"

"Nothing really. It's just something I've told Chase a hundred times. You're no good to anybody if you're dead . . .

including yourself. I hope to meet you soon in person, Rashawn. Have Chase call me when he gets back. And again, don't worry. He'll be fine. I've got to go now."

Rashawn put the phone back on the windowsill and looked over at Momma Rossi. She was still curled up on the hay bales sound asleep. Pet was swaying back and forth looking like a gray balloon ready to burst. The wind was still battering the barn but it didn't seem nearly as noisy to Rashawn.

"Maybe I'm getting used to the racket, or maybe I'm going deaf," she said to the elephant.

She walked past the light of Pet's ring into the dark.

I'll just poke my head outside and see what I can see.

Halfway to the door something bumped into her leg. She screamed. Pet trumpeted. Momma Rossi woke up.

"What is it, dear?"

Rashawn shined her flashlight at the ground. "It's a little green monkey no bigger than a squirrel."

"Poco!"

Momma Rossi ran over and gently scooped Poco up. The tiny monkey fit easily into the palms of her small hands.

"He's bleeding," Rashawn said.

"I see that. Let's get him to the ring."

In the light, they discovered that Poco's injuries were worse than they had first appeared. His right arm was broken and there was a gash on his back.

"There's a first aid kit hanging on the wall below the window," Momma Rossi said.

Rashawn ran over and got it.

"We're going to have to set his arm," Momma Rossi said. "Then we'll have to suture the wound and warm him up so he doesn't go into shock."

"Do you think he'll be okay?"

"I don't know. He's had a terrible night."

Chase and Nicole stood outside the third barn, or what was left of it. Two of its walls had collapsed and the roof was completely gone. There was no sign of the other lions. They had either escaped or were stuck under one of the walls. Chase hoped it was the latter.

"It's possible they're okay under there," he said. "There's a lot of hollow space. The side wall went down first, then the windward wall fell on top of it, forming a sort of a wind foil. See the angle?"

Nicole nodded.

"That might have protected them," Chase said.

Nicole pointed at the cage that had held Simba. The door was gone. "There's no doubt about how Simba got out."

"I hope he found another place to crawl into to get out of the rain," Chase said.

"He doesn't seem to be following us at the moment."

"You mean stalking us."

"I guess," Nicole said.

The wind had dropped off dramatically, but it was still raining hard, which meant the water was still rising. Chase was also worried about the barn where the Shack & Shop was parked. It might have collapsed too. He pulled his watch out of his pocket, surprised to see that they had been gone almost forty-five minutes.

Chase slipped the watch back onto his wrist, wincing at the pain in his shoulder.

"You okay?" Nicole asked.

"Yeah. My shoulder hurts a little in certain positions."

She gave him a doubtful look. "Like when you put your watch on?"

"I'll be fine. We need to keep moving. We've already been gone too long."

Nicole nodded and started toward the last barn. The rain pummeled them so hard they had to keep their heads down to breathe. The closer they got to the last barn, the deeper the water became. By the time they reached the door, the water was up to their knees.

"The barn's completely flooded," Nicole said.

"But it's still standing," Chase said. "Do lions like water?"

"No."

"Good. Let's get the gas and get out of here."

They waded inside, bumping debris away with their knees. Chase shined his light along the side of the fifth-wheel that he and his father had nicknamed the Shack. Water lapped against the bottom of the door.

"There's water inside," he said. "It's ruined." He looked at the side of the semitrailer they called the Shop. It sat higher than the fifth-wheel, so the water hadn't reached its threshold yet.

"We're going to have to move the Shop to higher ground," Chase said.

"You're kidding, right?"

"I'm serious."

"I thought we were in a hurry to get the gas back to the circus barn."

"We are. But along with the gas there's a hundred thousand dollars of tools and building supplies in there. If we leave the trailer here, we can kiss the contents good-bye."

"Do you know how to drive an eighteen-wheeler?" Nicole asked.

"I know how to start it, put it into gear, and step on the gas," Chase answered.

"And do you also know how to back one up?"

Tomás had pulled the semi into the barn tractor-first so they could get to the tools and supplies in the trailer easily.

"How hard can it be?" Chase said.

"A lot harder than going forward," Nicole said. "I'll drive."

"Now you're kidding?" Chase said.

"I'm a circus girl. I've been driving big rigs around the farm since I was eight."

"You couldn't even reach the pedals at eight," Chase protested.

"I was as tall as my father when I was eight," Nicole shot back.

"No offense," Chase said. "But your father isn't very tall."

"Exactly," Nicole said. "Neither is my mother or my grandmother. Which means every truck on the circus is equipped with pedal extenders, which is how I was able to drive a semi when I was eight years old. I *know* how to back a semi."

"Okay," Chase said. "You win. You're driving."

"We may not get very far with this much water on the ground," Nicole said.

"It can't be worse than leaving the rig where it is," Chase said. "I'll stand behind the trailer and flip on the headlamp's emergency flasher if you're going to slam into something. Are you sure you can do this?"

"I think so," Nicole answered, sounding a little less confident than she had a minute earlier. "I'll be okay if I can see your headlamp in the side mirror."

"The spare key's above the visor. Good luck."

They waded in opposite directions.

As Chase passed the fifth-wheel he wondered if there was anything he should grab before water got to it. He and his father had lived inside the Shack for two years. He couldn't think of one thing inside that could not be easily replaced at a Walmart. There were no photographs of his mother or sister, no mementos from the house they'd lived in before the accident, nothing from their past. Chase's father had told him that everything was in storage to protect it, but Chase wasn't convinced. He and his father rarely talked about their life before they started running toward storms.

It's as if we never had another life. As if we've always been on the —

His foot connected with something underwater and he fell forward with a splash. He got up choking on oily and gritty floodwater, one of his father's favorite sayings echoing in his head: *In an emergency you must focus. The moment you leave the moment could be the last moment of your life.*

Chase wiped away the water and grime from his face, along with any thoughts of his past.

Focus.

Nicole pulled open the heavy driver's door and clambered into the cab. It smelled like sweat, coffee, and fast food. She loved the scent. It reminded her of traveling with the circus — something she rarely got to do anymore because of school. She wondered if her mother even knew about Hurricane Emily. Probably not. With the show in Mexico, her mother was juggling a thousand tasks, made harder by being in a foreign country. She rarely called home when she was away because Nicole's father was notorious for misplacing his cell phone, running the battery dry, or turning the ringer off.

She pulled the visor down and the keys dropped into her lap. She made sure the semi was in park before putting the key into the ignition. The powerful diesel engine roared to life. She put on her seat belt, then adjusted the seat and side mirrors as the engine warmed.

Chase's headlamp looked like it was a mile away behind her.

"Here we go," she said. "Nice and slow. I don't want to run over my boyfriend. . . ."

Nicole blushed.

I haven't even known Chase for forty-eight hours. We're not boyfriend-girlfriend.

"Not yet," she said with a slight smile. "But I better slow that idea down too."

She took a deep breath, let it out, then eased the gear into reverse.

06:47 AM

"Marco thinks he knows a way to get us to the farm," John said.

Cindy, Mark, Richard, and Tomás were gathered next to the cot.

"I was going to try it myself," Marco said. "But I had a blowout. The police picked me up while I was changing the tire. I didn't want to go with them, but they threatened to slap the cuffs on me, so here I am. Frustrating. And now you tell me Hector's out. It can't get worse than that. He's the most dangerous animal we have on the farm."

"I did a report on him," Richard said.

"I saw it," Marco said. "But you don't know half the story about that cat. I should have never left my mother in the house by herself. I should have stayed on the farm and made sure the animals were secure."

"We need to get moving," John said.

"If we all try to leave at once, the police will try to stop us," Marco said. He looked at Richard. "Where's your van parked?"

"Out front."

"You need to pull it around back. There's an exit in the locker room the police aren't monitoring."

John held his hand out for the keys. "I'll drive."

Richard shook his head. "That's against company policy."

"I'm not driving," Cindy said.

"Neither am I," Mark said. "Not in this weather."

"I guess you'll have to take the wheel, Richard," Cindy said. "Have you ever driven in a hurricane?"

Richard tossed the keys to John. "If something happens, I was driving."

"Fine," John said, and gave the keys to Tomás.

They headed toward the locker room.

06:49 AM

"You think he'll be okay?" Rashawn asked.

Momma Rossi had managed to set Poco's arm with a makeshift splint made out of a tongue depressor. Then she'd laid him in a nest of hay and covered him with a dry towel to keep him warm.

"It's a miracle he's alive," Momma Rossi said. "Not many animals survive a leopard attack."

"When I saw him hanging all limp from that leopard's mouth last night, I thought for sure he was dead. I didn't even know what kind of farm this was. I thought I was seeing things."

"I wonder how Hector got out of his cage," Momma Rossi said.

"I hear you. I wonder how Poco got . . ." Rashawn looked out into the darkness. "The window."

"What are you talking about?"

"The broken window in the bunkhouse," Rashawn said, trying to keep her voice from shaking. "It's a good four feet off the ground. How'd Poco get through it with his arm all busted up?"

"He couldn't have," Momma Rossi said.

"Unless that leopard jumped through the window with him in his mouth," Rashawn said.

They both stared beyond the light with the same question: Was there a leopard staring back at them?

06:51 AM

Chase was walking back and forth several yards behind the semi, checking the clearance as Nicole reversed the rig in slow motion, when a strange feeling crept up the back of his neck. At first he ignored it, thinking it was cold rain running under his shirt collar, but the feeling persisted. He turned his head and froze. Simba was standing twenty feet behind him in water up to his golden belly.

Simba bared his yellowed teeth and roared.

I'm going to die, Chase thought. Slowly he reached up and switched off his headlamp, but he was far from invisible in the glow of the rig's taillights. Nicole continued to back the truck toward him. If he stayed put, the semi would run him over. If he moved, Simba would attack him.

I thought Nicole said cats don't like the water!

Simba looked as comfortable as a shark.

Why is Nicole still backing up? She can't see my headlamp. Why doesn't she stop? Why . . .

Chase realized that if Nicole stopped, the rig might lose momentum and get mired in the soft ground. He could see Simba clearly thanks to the taillights that were now only four feet away. His body was shouting RUN. But his brain was telling him to FREEZE.

Simba is just waiting for me to move.

Three feet.

Nicole continued to back up the truck at a steady rate. Chase slowly looked away from Simba and focused on the back of the trailer.

Two feet.

He put his arms out and laid his hands flat against the trailer doors.

One foot.

He felt the powerful truck push him over backward. He planted his feet and let the truck take him down into the water, which came nearly up to the undercarriage. He tried not to think of Simba's fangs sinking into his neck.

Concentrate. Keep your legs between the tires. Keep your head above the water.

He stretched his hands above his chest and let them play along the undercarriage until he found a strut he could grab. He felt his heels making furrows in the soft ground beneath the water as he was dragged along. A searing pain shot through his injured shoulder.

The trailer began to veer to the right.

She's cleared the barn. She's turning the rig so we have a straight shot to the circus barn. She's wondering where I am. Don't stop, Nicole! Keep cranking it!

The trailer stopped for a moment, then started forward. Chase managed to spin around so his heels were dragging again. The truck started to slow. Chase let go of the strut he'd been clinging to and rolled to his right, narrowly clearing the rear tires. He stumbled to his feet, wiping the water from his eyes in time to see the cab lights blink on as Nicole opened the door.

He splashed forward. "Stay in the cab!"

"What?"

"Simba!"

Nicole turned her headlamp on.

Chase glanced behind him and saw Simba come around the end of the trailer.

"You'll make it!" Nicole shouted.

Not if I trip or faint. Not if you slam the door.

Simba had cut the distance between them by half.

I'm not going to make it.

Nicole jumped out of the cab with the shotgun. She put it to her shoulder and pulled the trigger. A red flame came out of the barrel, followed by a deafening *BOOM*.

Chase glanced back at Simba. The lion was standing still, staring past him at Nicole. Chase threw himself into the cab, and Nicole clambered in next to him, slamming the door closed. A second later Simba's head appeared outside the passenger window. Nicole shrank back, practically landing in Chase's lap.

Simba roared, then his head disappeared.

Chase and Nicole stared at the window for a full minute before realizing they were both sitting in the passenger seat holding each other. Nicole flushed, then climbed back into the driver's seat.

"That was scary," she said.

Chase wondered if she was talking about them holding each other or the lion.

"It's still scary," he said. "Can he get in here?"

"No."

"Did you wound him?"

Nicole shook her head. "I fired into the water at his feet, or I guess his paws. It was enough to make him . . . pause."

"Funny."

"Where are your shoes?"

Chase looked down at his feet. Not only had he lost his shoes, but his socks had been pulled off too. "I guess they came off under the truck."

Nicole smiled. "Wanna try to find them?"

Chase smiled back. "Nah, I'm good."

Nicole released the brake and put the truck into gear.

06:59 AM

Tomás put the van into drive and pulled out of the high school parking lot. John was in the passenger seat with Marco sitting next to him. Cindy, Mark, and Richard were in the back, wedged between expensive television equipment.

Richard looked at Cindy and Mark. "Now that we're partners, let's take a look at that hurricane footage."

"Partners?" Mark asked.

Richard flashed his best anchorman smile. "Okay. How about colleagues, then? We still work for the same station."

"You told the boss that we resigned," Cindy pointed out.

"I can smooth out that misunderstanding."

"Maybe we don't want it smoothed out," Mark said.

"Whatever," Richard said. "We have nothing else to do. Let's see what you have."

Cindy nodded at Mark. He pulled a memory card out of his pocket and popped it into a laptop.

"How is it out there?" Cindy called up to John.

"Wet. Treacherous. But the rain has died down. I'd guess it's seventy miles an hour sustained, which puts Emily back into the tropical storm category. The bad news is that there's a lot of water on the road. The good news, at least for us, is that it's washing the lighter debris out of our way."

"This hurricane footage is fantastic!" Richard said. "We need to get it on the air right away."

"We'd have to stop to position the satellite dish," Mark said.

"Someplace with shelter," Cindy added. "This wind would rip the dish off the van."

"Turn right up ahead," Marco said.

"And pull over," Richard added.

"No," John said. "We're not here to get video on the air for the morning news. We have to get to the Rossis' farm."

Tomás turned the van right and ran over several small palmetto bushes.

"Is this even a road?" Richard said.

"Used to be," Marco answered. "They closed it down years ago after the highway opened. If we can get through, it will take us into Palm Breeze, and there are several ways to get to the farm from there."

"And if we can't?" Cindy asked.

"Then it's back to the shelter," John said. "This is our last shot."

07:02 AM

Chase looked out at the passenger side mirror. There was no sign of Simba, but that didn't mean the lion wasn't trotting behind the rig in the dark.

They had just reached the second barn, and Chase could see that another challenge was still ahead. To reach the circus barn they would have to drive across the water rushing between the two buildings.

"Stop here," he said.

"Why?"

"Just stop for a second."

Nicole stepped on the brake and took the truck out of gear. "What's the matter? We're almost there. It's only fifty yards away."

"It might as well be fifty miles away," Chase said. "Look at the water in front of us."

"I see it," Nicole said. "It doesn't look nearly as wide as it was before."

"But it's moving faster now and I'm guessing that's because it's deeper."

"I think we can make it across," Nicole said. "If we get bogged down, we'll still be closer to the barn."

"This rig is worth a lot of money. To say nothing about the stuff inside the trailer."

"What do you want to do?"

"I think we should get that gas out of the back and wade across. If we find that it's not too deep, we can get back in and drive across instead."

"You're barefoot," Nicole said.

"I'll have to be careful where I step."

"And Simba is out there."

"Believe me," Chase said. "I'd rather drive too. And if we could get the rig there, I might be able to hook up the two generators we have in back to the barn. We'd have power for a week. But if the truck gets stuck, we might lose everything inside."

Chase looked at his watch. They had been gone for more than an hour. He wondered if the generator in the barn was still working.

07:04AM

Inside the circus barn, the lights flickered and then went out.

Pet trumpeted. Rashawn screamed.

Momma Rossi put her hand on Rashawn's arm and said, "Be calm, dear."

"Sorry," Rashawn said. "It's embarrassing but I'm kind of afraid of the dark. Add a leopard to that and I'm petrified."

"We don't know if Hector's out there," Momma Rossi said. "You said you closed the bunkhouse door when you came back into the barn."

"I did," Rashawn said. "But it was open the whole time Chase and I were in there. Hector could have slipped into the barn anytime."

"We've already been over this," Momma Rossi said. "You and Chase didn't see Hector in the bunkhouse."

Rashawn took a deep breath to calm herself. "No, ma'am, we didn't, but he could have gone through the door when we weren't looking."

"Right," Momma Rossi said. "But if he had, it means he was more interested in getting into the barn than he was in attacking you and Chase."

"I guess," Rashawn said.

"You're standing here. No scratches that I can see."

"It's dark," Rashawn said. "We can't see anything."

Momma Rossi laughed. "You know what I mean, Rashawn."

"What are we going to do now?"

"There's nothing we can do for Pet without light. So as a precaution, and it's just a precaution, I think we should head down to the cat cage. It's made to keep the cats in, but it will work just as well to keep a cat out. I'm going to let your arm go. Do you think you can find the flashlight?"

"I think so. I'm trying to remember where I saw it before the lights went out."

"Be careful not to stumble over Poco. And whatever you do, don't step into the ring with Pet."

"Are you afraid that ol' elephant might punch me out?"

"No, I'm afraid that she might kill you."

"You're not kidding, are you?" Rashawn said. "I guess it'd be a shame to be killed by a pregnant pachyderm after surviving the storm of the century."

07:06 AM

Chase and Nicole sloshed to the end of the trailer in water up to their calves. Nicole took the lead with the shotgun. Chase followed, keeping an eye out from behind, with his bare feet numbed by the cold water.

"Anything?" Nicole asked.

"Trust me," Chase said. "I'll scream if I see a lion."

"We're almost there."

Nicole stopped. Chase bumped into her. Neither of them laughed.

"I'm going to step out from the trailer and circle around for a wider view. Watch my back."

"Sure," Chase said, although he had no idea what he could do to protect her from a lion attack.

When they had climbed out of the truck, Chase had taken the tranquilizer pistol out of his cargo pocket. Nicole had told him to put it back. She'd said that it would only work at close range. "Also, tranquilizer darts only work fast in the movies," she'd added. "In real life, it can take twenty minutes for an animal to go down."

Nicole slowly stepped around the trailer with the shotgun ready. She and Chase shined their headlamps back and forth through the darkness. Simba was not there.

"Let's get the gas and get out of here," Nicole said.

Chase released the latch, swung the door open, and switched on the interior lights.

"Wow," Nicole said.

"Yeah," Chase agreed, looking at the well-organized workshop running almost the entire length of the trailer. He pointed at the far end. "That door past the workbench and tools leads to Tomás's apartment."

"But there's a sleeper in the truck."

"Not very comfortable as permanent sleeping quarters."

Chase climbed into the trailer and made his way to the generator while Nicole watched from the door. There were two five-gallon gas cans next to it. He picked them both up, but immediately dropped one as pain shot to his right shoulder.

I can't carry both of them, Chase thought. *And I can't let Nicole carry the other. She needs both her hands for the shotgun.*

He walked back to the door with one can.

Nicole stood on the ground with her elbows resting on the trailer floorboards. She looked as if she were about ready to fall asleep.

"I thought there were two cans," she said wearily.

"One will do. It'll keep us going for hours. We can come back and get the other one when it gets —"

Simba was airborne and flying right at him.

Chase dove down toward Nicole and pushed her to the side. Simba hit the shop floor ten feet past him and slid. Chase rolled out of the trailer and managed to land on his feet. He caught the edge of the door and slammed it shut just as Simba turned around and started his second charge.

Chase jammed the locking bolt into place and stumbled backward. His knees buckled. He sat down in six inches of water, hyperventilating.

"Why did you knock me down?" Nicole asked indignantly.

Chase couldn't inhale enough air into his lungs to answer her. His heart was beating so hard he thought it was going to explode.

Simba hit the door from inside and roared. The door rattled but held.

Nicole jumped back from the trailer, then stared at Chase. "How did —"

Chase held his hand up for her to wait and slowly got to his feet. He took a couple of deep breaths. "I didn't knock you down for the fun of it. You missed the leaping lion act. It was pretty spectacular."

"What are you talking about?" Nicole said.

"I saw Simba leaping toward the trailer. I pushed you down and rolled out. I don't know how I got the door closed behind me. It all happened so fast. If you blinked, you would have missed it."

"Lucky you didn't blink," Nicole said.

Chase almost wished he had. The image of Simba flying over his head was going to haunt him for the rest of his life. "I blew it," he said. "The gas can." He looked at the trailer door. "I'm not going back in there to get it."

"You don't have to." Nicole reached under the trailer and picked up the can. "It must have fallen out when you jumped."

The trailer door rattled again. "What do you think he's doing in there?" Chase asked.

"Looking for a way out."

07:09 AM

Rashawn and Momma Rossi slowly made their way toward the big cat cage at the far end of the circus barn. Rashawn held the flashlight. Momma Rossi held Poco.

Eyeshine, Rashawn thought. *Yellow. I think.*

Rashawn's father had taught her a lot about *tapetum lucidum,* or eyeshine, in animals. One of her favorite things to do was drive around with him at night spotlighting wildlife. One of her father's responsibilities as refuge manager was to determine which animals lived on the refuge. Raccoon, dog, and cat eyes reflected yellow light. Rashawn and her father could tell what an animal was by the height of its eyes off the ground and by how far apart they were.

She swept the flashlight back and forth. "I just hope that two yellow eyes don't shine back at me."

"What's that, dear?" Momma Rossi asked.

"Just talking to myself. I do that when I'm nervous."

"I'm nervous too," Momma Rossi admitted. "But I think we'll be fine. We're halfway there. If Hector was in the —"

Rashawn had stopped. The beam of her flashlight shined on two yellow eyes and a spotted face.

"Oh my," Momma Rossi whispered.

"What do we do?" Rashawn whispered back.

"No matter what your legs are telling you," Momma Rossi said firmly, "do not run."

That was exactly what Rashawn's legs were telling her to do. The only thing stopping her was the fact that there was nowhere to run to. Hector was crouched in front of the cat cage, blocking their way to the bunkhouse and the door Chase and Nicole had used to leave the barn. There was the door behind them, but Rashawn doubted they could get to it before the leopard got to them.

"I'll take the flashlight. You take Poco," Momma Rossi said.

"What's the plan?"

"I want you to head over to the ladder by the flier ring and climb up to the platform."

"Aren't leopards good climbers?" Rashawn asked.

"They are, but they have to have something to sink their claws into. The ladder is made out of metal. Do you think you can get up there holding Poco?"

"I think so."

"Good." Momma Rossi took the flashlight and gently handed Poco to her. "I'll shine the light on the ladder until you start up. Do you think you'll have a problem climbing in the dark?"

"I should be okay," Rashawn said. "If I run into a snag, I'll tell you and you can switch it on behind me."

"Oh, I won't be behind you, dear."

"Huh?"

"I'll stay down here and distract Hector while you get up to that platform."

"No way," Rashawn said.

"There's no time to debate," Momma Rossi said. "I'm too old to climb that ladder. I've been working with cats since I was a little girl. I can save myself, but I don't think I can save all three of us. Now go!"

Rashawn went, but she didn't feel right about it. As soon as she grabbed the first rung, Momma Rossi swung the flashlight beam away. Climbing in the pitch dark with an injured monkey in the crook of her arm was nearly impossible. Ten feet up Rashawn was sweating and out of breath. She paused and looked down — and what she saw nearly caused her to fall off the ladder. Hector was batting the flashlight around the floor like a cat torturing a mouse.

The beam went out.

"Momma Rossi?" Rashawn shouted. "Momma Rossi?"

There was no answer.

07:15 AM

"Stop here," John said.

Tomás pulled the van over to what might have been the curb, though it was difficult to tell under a foot of water. They had reached the town of Palm Breeze.

"I want to check something out," John said. "It will only take a minute." He got out of the van, and Tomás and Marco joined him.

"Let's see if we can beam some of this video to the station," Richard said.

"What do you think?" Mark asked Cindy.

"I guess it won't hurt," Cindy answered. "But I want to be on camera."

"We'll both do the stand-up," Richard said.

"Fine."

They started putting the gear together while Mark set up the satellite dish.

John, Tomás, and Marco waded over to a building. John shined his flashlight on the sign.

"Palm Breeze Middle School," Marco said. "All my kids have gone here."

There was wind and water damage to the main building, but it was in pretty good shape compared to some of the other buildings they had passed driving through town. They wandered farther into the school complex.

Marco pointed. "That's the cafetorium."

They walked over and John shined his flashlight through the window. "Dry as a bone," he said. "That's the strange thing about storm surge. You never know how the water is going to flow."

"And hindsight is perfect," Marco said.

"Yep," John agreed. "But I still think Dr. Krupp should have kept the kids here rather than putting them on a bus. This cafeteria is a good five feet above the buildings in front."

"She'll figure it out when she gets back to school," Marco said.

Just then, Tomás's satellite phone rang, which was odd, because the only person who ever called him on it was John. He took it out of his coat pocket and answered. *"¿Qué pasa?"*

"Chase?" John asked.

Tomás shook his head gravely. "No."

"How about if we upload all your raw footage and let them edit it at the station?" Richard suggested.

"Here we go," Mark muttered to Cindy.

"I heard that," Richard said. "I'm not trying to steal anything from you. You'll get all of the credit. Our viewers want to know what happened during Hurricane Emily. We have an obligation to tell them. I'll make sure you get the video rights after we air it."

"Fine," Cindy said. "But we need to get moving. I don't know what they're off looking at, but when John's finished he'll want to get back on the road."

They climbed out of the back of the van.

"Palm Breeze Middle School," Richard said. "What's John looking at here?"

"Who knows," Cindy said. "At one point last night he and Tomás got down on their bellies to see how a road disintegrates in a Category Five hurricane."

"What's the matter with him?"

Cindy laughed. "John's a little different."

"Who was it?" John asked.

Tomás put the satellite phone back into his pocket, then launched into a long explanation in Spanglish.

"More bad news." John turned to Marco. "That was Tomás's brother."

"Arturo?"

John nodded. "He was calling from Mexico City. He drove ahead of the show to set things up for the next date. Unfortunately, the show didn't show up."

"Where are they?"

"He doesn't know exactly. No one is answering their cell phones. He thinks they're outside a city called Puebla."

"How late are they?"

"Twenty-four hours."

"How far is Puebla from Mexico City?"

"It's only seventy miles, but that's not the problem. There's been an earthquake in Puebla. A big one. The city's a disaster area. And it gets worse." John glanced at Tomás. "Twenty-five miles east of Puebla is an active volcano called Popocatepetl. Tomás's family lives in a small village on the side of that mountain."

07:23 AM

"At least it's starting to get light out here," Nicole said.

"And the wind has dropped even more," Chase added. "We might just live through this storm."

"You had doubts?"

Chase smiled. "You didn't?"

They had just waded across the gap. The water in the deepest part had been up to their waists. The semi would never have made it across.

"After we get the generator filled, will you try to reach your dad?" Nicole asked.

"If the phone works," Chase answered, opening the door.

"Dark," Nicole said.

"I wonder how long they've been out of gas."

They stepped inside and closed the door behind them.

"Hello?" Nicole called.

The only thing they heard was Pet pulling on her chain.

"You think they're out looking for us?" Chase asked.

"Hector's in the barn!" Rashawn's warning echoed through the metal barn.

"Where?" Nicole shouted back.

"Don't know. I'm up on the flier platform. I don't know where Momma Rossi is either. I think she's hiding down there somewhere. She can't answer back because it'll give her hiding place away. At least I think that's the situation."

"Stay where you are," Nicole said.

Chase sliced his headlamp through the darkness. "How did Hector get in here?"

"I don't know, but we need to get the lights on. We need to find Momma Rossi," Nicole said.

"You think she's hiding like Rashawn said."

"I hope so. Let's get gas in the generator."

Chase hesitated. "Rashawn is safe up there," he said. "And Momma Rossi might be fine too. The weather isn't too bad. Maybe we should go back outside and wait for help. At least that way *we'll* be safe from Hector."

"No," Nicole said.

"I knew you were going to say that, but could you just think about it for a second?"

"I'll think about it in the bunkhouse," Nicole said.

"Okay."

Chase was glad to see that the bunkhouse door was closed, which meant that Hector could not have sneaked inside. They slipped through, securing the door behind them, then hurried past the apartments to the shop.

"How long will the generator run?" Nicole asked as he filled the tank.

"Several hours. Depends on how many lights we turn on out in the barn. What's your plan?"

"Hector can't get up to the platform where Rashawn is hiding. She's safe. We have to find Momma Rossi and make sure she's okay, then we have to contain Hector."

Chase put the lid back on the tank, pulled the choke out, and pushed the start button. The generator started purring. He turned to Nicole. "Could you be a little more specific about your plan?"

"I need to show you how to use that tranquilizer gun," Nicole said.

When the light over Pet's ring came on, Rashawn's first instinct was to climb down and join Chase and Nicole in the bunkhouse, but two things held her back. One was Hector. The other was Poco. She couldn't take him with her.

"Dodging a leopard while carrying a monkey is a very bad idea," she said firmly.

She couldn't leave Poco behind, though. There were no edges on the platform. He might roll off, and, with a broken arm, probably wouldn't survive the fall.

"Even if he's lucky enough to land in that catch net," she said, peering over the edge of the platform into the darkness, trying to find Momma Rossi's hiding spot, or a spotted leopard slinking in the shadows. She saw neither. The only thing moving below was Pet.

"Hector can't take that big ol' elephant down. But if she starts to have her baby, he might be able to. . . ."

The satellite phone rang from its spot on the windowsill.

No one could reach it.

*   *   *

"No answer?" Marco sounded sick with worry.

"No answer," John confirmed. "How soon do you think we'll be there?"

"Fifteen minutes if we don't run into a snag."

John stared through the windshield. The rain had all but stopped, the wind had dropped, and the storm surge seemed to be receding, but the damage had already been done. Palm Breeze was ruined. It would take months, if not years, to recover from Hurricane Emily. There would be a lot of work.

"But not for us," John said.

"What?" Marco asked.

"Sorry," John said. "Just thinking out loud." He turned and looked at Cindy and Mark. "Do either of you speak Spanish?"

"Nope," Mark said.

"*Un poco,*" Cindy answered. "A little."

He hadn't yet told them about Tomás's conversation with his brother, Arturo. Or the change in plan.

"Two darts," Nicole said. "Two chances."

"At fifty feet," Chase said.

"Or less. The darts aren't very accurate past fifty. Aim for a big muscle like the meaty part of his hind leg."

"How long does it take a leopard to cover fifty feet?"

"About as long as it took Simba to jump into the truck over your head."

"That's pretty quick."

"I can do this on my own," Nicole said. "I mean it, Chase. There's no reason for us both to risk our hides."

"I think I have a little more experience with big cat attacks than you do." Chase smiled. "Now."

"Ha," Nicole said. "Here's how we'll handle it. If I think he's going to pounce, I'll fire the shotgun. It will sound like a nuclear bomb inside the barn."

"Louder," Chase said. His ears were still ringing from when she shot the ostrich.

"Hopefully the sound will be enough to get him to back off."

"What if the nuclear explosion doesn't work?"

"I guess I'll have to shoot him."

"How many bullets do you have?"

"They're called shells," Nicole corrected. "And I have plenty."

The only gun Chase had ever fired was his father's nail gun.

They headed to the door with Nicole in the lead. Before they stepped into the barn, she unhooked a fire extinguisher from the wall and handed it to him.

"Good idea," he said. "We can put Hector out if he catches on fire."

"Funny."

"Seriously. What do you want me to do with this?"

"Big cats are cautious," Nicole said. "Simba backed off when I fired the shotgun because he'd never seen or heard one before. It probably wouldn't work a second time. I doubt Hector has seen a fire extinguisher in use. It'll stop him in his tracks."

"Once," Chase said.

Nicole nodded. "Once."

They stepped into the dark circus barn.

Rashawn heard the door open and saw Chase's and Nicole's headlamps.

"What are you doing?" she shouted. "I told you Hector's in here."

"Have you seen him since we left?" Nicole shouted back.

"No."

"Momma Rossi?"

"Not a sign."

"Stay where you are. We're going to find her. Keep your eyes open. If you see Hector, tell —"

"Don't worry," Rashawn said. "You'll be the first to know. By the way . . . Poco is alive. I have him up here with me."

"Maybe Hector isn't as aggressive as we think," Chase said hopefully.

"Don't count on it," Nicole said. "Momma Rossi? I hope you can hear me. Chase and I are coming to get you. I have the shotgun. Chase has the tranquilizer pistol."

"I hope Hector doesn't understand English," Rashawn shouted from her perch.

"Funny," Nicole said.

"I hope she's right," Chase said.

"Watch for eyeshine," Rashawn yelled. "Yellow eyes."

"Yellow eyes," Chase repeated. "I hope we don't see them."

"I hope we do," Nicole said. "Before they see us."

They moved away from the safety of the door. With each footstep into the huge barn Chase's anxiety grew. Every shadow looked like an enraged leopard.

"We'll stay in the middle of the barn so we have time to react," Nicole whispered. "I'll look to the right, you look to the left."

"What about our backs?" Chase asked.

"We'll go slow and make sure we don't walk past him."

This didn't seem like a very good plan to Chase, but he kept it to himself. "Do you have any idea where Momma Rossi might be hiding?"

"I'm pretty sure she isn't in a very secure place, or she would have answered us by now," Nicole said.

"Which means that Hector knows where we are because we're talking," Chase said.

"Hector knows where we are because we're *here*," Nicole said. "Our job is to distract him so he doesn't find Momma Rossi. We're the mice."

"Mice with guns," Chase said.

"And a fire extinguisher," Nicole added.

07:43 AM

"This is as far as we go," John said.

The group was standing in front of the van, looking at water gushing through a wide gap where the road to the farm used to be.

"We're only a couple hundred yards from the front gate," Marco said. "The fence is down. Looks like if we follow this stream up on this side, we'll end up near the barns."

"That might save us from wading across," John said.

"Wait a second," Richard protested. "Are you suggesting that we head out on foot?"

"How else are we going to get to the farm?" John asked.

"There's a leopard running around."

"That's probably not all that's running around," Marco said.

"I appreciate your letting us use the van," John said. "You can wait here or you can drive back to the shelter." He looked at Cindy and Mark. "That goes for you two as well. You might want to stay here until it's safe."

"Safe?" Mark said. "Since when have you been worried about our safety?"

"Good point," Cindy said.

John grinned. "I know a lot about big storms, but I don't know anything about big cats — except that they scare me."

"John Masters scared?" Cindy said. "This I've got to see. I'm going with you."

"Me too," Mark said.

Richard sighed but joined them as they filed past the fence into the soggy paddock.

As they climbed, John tried Chase's phone again.

07:45 AM

"The sat phone!" Chase said.

"It's probably your dad," Rashawn shouted down. "He's called a couple of times."

The phone continued ringing. Chase wanted to run through Pet's ring and answer it, but that would surely draw Hector's attention. He and Nicole continued their slow walk down the center of the barn.

"Where is he?" Chase asked.

"He's on his way here. And he found Nicole's dad."

"Thank goodness. Is he okay?" Nicole shouted.

"Yes. He's with Chase's dad."

The phone rang five more times, then went silent.

"Maybe we should wait for them," Chase said.

"On the way and getting here are two different things," Nicole said.

Chase knew she was right. They were midway down the center of the long barn. Getting back to the bunkhouse door would take just as long as continuing on to the elephant ring. The only difference was that Hector wasn't behind them.

"Hopefully," Chase said.

"What?" Nicole asked.

"Nothing. Let's get this squeeze play over with."

"Guys?" Rashawn called out quietly.

Her change in tone stopped both Nicole and Chase in midstep. They swung their headlamps back and forth frantically, trying to see what she had seen. Nicole tracked her headlamp's beam with the shotgun. Chase held up the fire extinguisher in one hand and the tranquilizer pistol in the other while turning a complete three-sixty.

"Look at Pet," Nicole said.

She was standing perfectly still with her ears flared and her trunk in the air. "What's she doing?"

"She's looking up," Nicole answered.

They tilted their heads back. Thirty feet above them was a series of catwalks, and slinking down the one directly above them was a leopard.

"How did he get up there?" Chase asked.

"He climbed up on these bales of hay," Momma Rossi said, rushing out from behind the stack. "That's why I couldn't answer you."

Hector was less than twenty feet away from Rashawn.

"Shoot him," Chase said.

"I can't," Nicole said. "He's too close to Rashawn."

"Use the ladder, Rashawn!" Chase shouted.

"No time," Momma Rossi said. "Jump!"

07:46AM

"Are you kidding?" Rashawn shouted. "I can't even see the net in the dark!"

"Relax your body," Momma Rossi called up to her. "Land on your back."

"That's easy for you to say! Sorry, ma'am. I don't mean to be rude, but it's true!" Rashawn looked along the catwalk. Hector stalked toward her in the flickering headlamp lights.

She turned her back to him, got down on her knees on the edge of the platform, and scooped Poco into her arms.

"This is stupid," she said, then rolled off the platform into the air.

Rashawn felt her stomach lurch into her throat. She couldn't tell if she was falling backward, frontward, or headfirst.

Hector leapt for the platform just as Rashawn dropped into the darkness below.

Momma Rossi reached the net before Rashawn's second bounce. "Roll!"

Rashawn was horrified to see that Hector was ten feet away from her, trying to regain his footing. She rolled.

Nicole yanked the pistol from Chase's hand and ran under the net. He rushed forward to help Rashawn.

"Take Poco," Rashawn said.

He gently took the little monkey from her and stepped back as she did a backward somersault off the net.

Pop.

Hector jumped up in the air, snarling.

Nicole came out from under the net. "I think I got the dart in."

"He's not too happy about it," Chase said.

"What dart?" Rashawn asked.

"Tranquilizer dart," Nicole explained.

Hector was trying to pull the dart from his hind leg with his teeth.

"His claws are snagged in the net," Rashawn said. "He's getting tangled up."

"Perfect," Momma Rossi said. "Let's put the cat in the bag before he gets untangled."

"What about the tranquilizer?" Rashawn asked.

"It takes a few minutes for it to take effect," Momma Rossi explained.

"Hector can do a lot of damage in a few seconds," Nicole added. She looked at Momma Rossi. "Do you want to fold it up like we do in the show?"

"Yes, but we'll have to do it a lot quicker," Momma Rossi said.

"What are you talking about?" Chase asked.

"Watch," Nicole said.

"Can I borrow your headlamp?" Momma Rossi asked.

Chase handed Poco to Rashawn and took the headlamp off. Once Momma Rossi had the headlamp over her gray hair, she and Nicole went to the far end of the catch net and took up positions on opposite corners.

"Ready?" Momma Rossi called out.

"Yes."

"On three. One . . . two . . . three!"

The end of the net dropped to the ground. They picked up their corners and hurried forward, pulling the net over the top of the struggling leopard. When they had the net halved, they brought it back, quartering it, and so on until the net was about four feet wide. They flipped the ends up and stood back, panting and admiring their work.

"Leopard in a cube," Rashawn said.

"He's already starting to slow down," Nicole said. "We should be able to unwrap him and haul him to the cat cage in a few minutes."

"How's Poco?" Momma Rossi asked.

"The thirty-foot drop doesn't seem to have hurt him," Rashawn said, placing Poco gently into his owner's small hands.

"How are *you*?" Nicole asked Rashawn.

"It wasn't nearly as bad as I thought it would be. But I don't want to do it again. Ever."

"I guess the drama's over," Momma Rossi said.

Chase looked at his watch. Had it really been just twenty-four hours since he'd stepped into Palm Breeze Middle School?

Pet trumpeted, and they all turned to her ring. The drama was not over.

07:57 AM

Momma Rossi and Rashawn had rushed back to Pet's ring. Chase waited with Nicole to help her carry Hector to the cat cage. They started carefully peeling away the net.

"How will you know he's out?" Chase asked.

"Gentle prodding," Nicole said.

She found a broom and unscrewed the handle. Each time they pulled a layer off, she tapped Hector on the head and waited. If there was no reaction, they removed another layer.

"One layer left," Nicole said.

They could see Hector clearly now through the fine mesh. His eyes and mouth were open. Nicole touched him several times around his ears and muzzle, waiting for a reaction.

"I think he's down for the count," she said.

They pulled the last layer off. Hector didn't move.

"Now what?" Chase asked.

"We pick him up and carry him to the cage."

"Have you ever had one wake up while you're carrying it?"

"I've never picked up an immobilized cat before."

"That's encouraging."

"But I've seen it done a half a dozen times. I've never seen one wake up."

"Let's hope your perfect record isn't broken this morning."

Hector wasn't heavy, but carrying him was awkward, and painful for Chase's bad shoulder. Nicole took the head and front legs, Chase took the hind legs, and they shuffled their way to the big cage. They were halfway there when the door to the barn opened, and they were blinded by several flashlight beams.

Marco was the first to reach them.

"Dad!" Nicole shouted.

"I'd give you a hug, but I see you have your hands full. Is he dead?"

"Tranquilized."

John, Tomás, Cindy, Mark, and Richard joined them.

"You okay?" John asked, staring at the leopard.

"We're fine," Chase said.

John grinned. "Guess you had an eventful night."

Chase returned the grin. "You might say that."

"Need a hand?"

"Yeah, my shoulder got banged up."

Tomás stepped forward and took Hector all by himself. "Where?"

"Follow me," Marco said.

John introduced everyone as they followed Tomás and Marco.

"We'll put him into one of the holding cages," Marco said,

sliding open a guillotine door. "It will be easier to deal with him in here after the drug wears off."

Tomás laid Hector inside on a bed of straw.

"Is that you, Marco?" Momma Rossi hollered from the other end of the barn.

"Yes, Momma," he hollered back, then looked at Nicole. "Sounds like your grandmother isn't any the worse for wear." He closed the door.

"You'd better hurry," Momma Rossi called. "I think your elephant is about ready to have her calf."

08:15 AM

Everyone had gathered around the elephant ring, waiting. Mark had started his camera rolling.

"It's kind of dark in here," John observed. "We have some spare generators in our trailer. Tomás and I could go and —"

"Not a good idea, Dad," Chase said.

"Why not? The weather's fine now."

"That's not the problem," Chase said. "There's a lion locked in the trailer."

"What?"

About halfway through his explanation about how Simba had gotten into the Shop, Pet gave birth.

The calf emerged with a whoosh of fluid, hitting the hay-covered floor hard enough to break the pinkish embryonic sac. The tiny calf started kicking immediately. Pet whipped around. For a moment it looked as if she was going to step on the calf, but then she nudged it gently with her foot. She reached down with her trunk and pulled away some of the sac from its wrinkled gray skin.

"I had no idea elephants had that much hair when they were born," Richard said.

"I didn't either," Cindy said.

The calf struggled to get up, but couldn't seem to get its long legs under its body.

"Is it a male or female?" Nicole asked.

"We won't be able to figure that out for a while," Marco answered.

"It looks strong," Rashawn said.

"And more important," Momma Rossi said, "Pet looks calm."

Marco nodded. "You're right. I haven't seen her this tranquil in weeks. She might just take care of this calf." He looked at Nicole. "What do you think we should name it?"

Nicole thought for a minute. "If it's a girl, I think we should call her Emily." She looked at Chase. "What should we call it if it's a boy?"

Chase smiled.

"Storm."

08:42 AM

The calf finally managed to get to its feet and take a few wobbly steps.

Tomás had pulled several bales of hay around the ring for everyone to sit on. Chase shared a bale with his father. Rashawn sat with Tomás. Richard with Cindy. Nicole was squeezed between Marco and Momma Rossi. Mark was not sitting. He was darting around the ring, videotaping Pet and her calf.

"Tell me about your shoulder," Chase's father said.

Chase described their desperate run across the crumbling levee road the previous day.

His father shook his head in wonder. "We saw you."

"What are you talking about?"

"Your headlamps on the other end of the washed-out road. Of course we didn't know it was *you*. Mark caught it on video."

Chase rubbed his sore shoulder. "You wouldn't have been able to reach us. By then, the levee was gone."

His father nodded. "We'll have to get your shoulder checked out."

"I need to go to the dentist," Chase said, showing him his broken front tooth.

"We'll take care of that too," his father said, then looked across the ring at the calf.

Something wasn't right. His father wasn't asking the *questions*. After every storm there was a debriefing. They would go over the disaster in minute detail, point by point, discussing what they had done, and what they should have done. His father was exhausted — they were all exhausted — but that had never stopped him before.

"What's going on?" Chase asked.

His father looked at him with sad eyes. "Earthquake. A big one in Mexico. It's near Tomás's family. Nicole's mom and the circus are in the same area. They're off the grid. We can't reach them by phone."

"Does Nicole know?"

"I doubt that Marco has had time to tell her, or his mother."

The calf took some tentative steps underneath Pet. It put its tiny trunk over its head and opened its mouth.

"It's nursing," Nicole said happily.

"What are we going to do?" Chase asked quietly.

His father stood up. "We're going to Mexico."

STORM RUNNERS
ERUPTION

ROLAND SMITH
AUTHOR OF *CRYPTID HUNTERS* AND *TENTACLES*

ABOUT THE AUTHOR

Roland Smith is the author of numerous award-winning books for young readers, including *Zach's Lie*, *Jack's Run*, *Cryptid Hunters*, *Peak*, *I, Q*, and *Tentacles*. For more than twenty years, he worked as an animal keeper, traveling all over the world, before turning to writing full-time. Roland lives with his wife, Marie, on a small farm south of Portland, Oregon. Visit him online at www.rolandsmith.com.